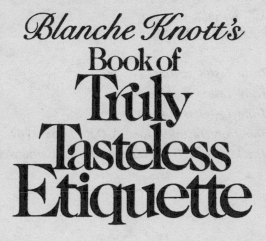

Blanche Knott's
Book of
Truly
Tasteless
Etiquette

Blanche Knott's
Book of
Truly
Tasteless
Etiquette

ST. MARTIN'S PRESS/NEW YORK

BLANCHE KNOTT'S BOOK OF TRULY TASTELESS ETIQUETTE

Copyright © 1987 by Blanche Knott

Published by arrangement with the author.

ISBN: 0-312-90590-4   Can. ISBN: 0-312-90591-2

Printed in the United States of America

First St. Martin's Press mass market edition/April 1987

10 9 8 7 6 5 4 3 2 1

For Tom—
Neil owes it all to him anyway

I don't acknowledge any help from anyone.

These are all my own ideas and anyone who disagrees can take it up with my lawyer.

—Blanche Knott
New York City, 1987

CONTENTS

I. Special Occasions

II. Around the House

III. Out and About

IV. Especially Delicate Social Matters

I would not enter on my list of friends,
(Though graced with polish'd manners
*   and fine sense,*
Yet wanting sensibility), the man
Who needlessly sets foot upon a worm.

—WILLIAM COWPER

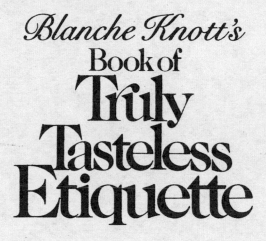

Blanche Knott's
Book of
**Truly
Tasteless
Etiquette**

PART I

Special Occasions

Who's kidding whom when today's bride walks down the aisle wearing white? Why do we spend so much time worrying about what to wear at a funeral when the guest of honor is dead? Why do we have showers with no water? Are divorce parties appropriate? Whose idea was it to slice off a chunk of a baby's dick? And why do we spend a lot of money on crappy holiday gifts for people we don't like?

Special occasions, when people are drawn together to celebrate or commiserate—whether they want to or not—are a lot like a hockey game. We all try to skate through with a minimum of hassle and an eye on the goal. We stay away from the "body checks," and have as few "face-offs" as possible. And when a confrontation or question of behavior rears its ugly head, there's got to be a referee to keep the combatants from killing each other. Off the ice these rules are known as etiquette.

At least in hockey, the refs wait a couple of minutes before breaking up a good fight. This is a good lesson to keep in mind off the ice. You can't escape the basic tenets of comportment I'm going to set out—so get in a few licks before you go down.

Coming of Age

Coming of age, when little jerkoffs move toward big jerkoff status, involves phenomena of grave social import. Life would be much simpler if, like certain African tribes, our young achieved adulthood by hunting down a wild beast and killing it with their bare hands. I'd be satisfied if the brats went after cats and small dogs.

Instead, we make a big deal over splashing babies with water or snipping away at their little dicks, not to mention pissing away colossal sums of money on the kid's thirteenth, sixteenth, and eighteenth birthdays. (I really pity those Jews who end up spending loads of dough on their JAPy daughters; they're constantly coming of one age or another.) Why don't we follow the lead of our black brothers? By the time those kids are thirteen, the father's split and they've already learned how to mug honkies so they don't have to bother mom for spending money. But if you insist on sticking to the conventional rituals, here are some pointers.

Q. I know this must be a silly question and doesn't quite pertain to etiquette, but I don't want to look the fool when our rabbi circumcises our son. What does he use to perform this delicate operation?

A. A bris-kit.

•

Q. Our rabbi is scheduled to circumcise our son next week and I'd like to have a small celebration afterwards with some close friends and family. What should I serve at the reception?

A. See answer above.

•

Q. I've been feeling very guilty lately because I haven't taken my job as a godparent seriously. How can I make amends?

A. Don't blow a good thing. Maintain that low profile and you'll be spared expensive yearly duties.

•

Q. My wife and I aren't very religious, but we'd like to baptize our child in some secular way. Can this be done?

A. Yes. Use the tub.

•

Q. What are the godparents' responsibilities?

A. Not to drop the baby during the service.

•

Q. We've been invited to attend the baptism of a Mexican friend's baby. What sort of gift should we bring?

A. Bean dip.

•

Q. Who should hold the baby during the christening?

A. Toss it up and call it in the air.

•

Q. What's the difference between a bar mitzvah and a bat mitzvah?

A. The "r" and the "t." That wasn't so difficult, was it?

•

Q. I am a little nervous about my upcoming sweet sixteen party. Are the guests going to expect anything special from me?

A. Proof of your virginity.

•

Q. Exactly what is a debut, and should we plan one for our sixteen-year-old daughter? We are new in town and I want to do the right thing.

A. The debut is a series of parties given to indicate officially that a girl is of marriageable age. Unless your daughter is unusually ugly, she will undoubtedly have become intimately acquainted with lots of the local boys, and by the time she turns eighteen they won't even *consider* marrying her. Spend your money on a college far from home—she'll be able to outrun her reputation, or at least acquire some useful job skills.

•

Q.   How much does a coming-out party usually cost?

A.   How much is your daughter's reputation worth?

•

Q.   How should a debutante deport herself?

A.   She should find a friendly country that will accept her. Check with Immigration for details.

•

Q.   Since I've gone through menopause and want nothing to do with sex, would it be appropriate to give my daughter my old diaphragm? She has just reached her twelfth birthday.

A.   Are you kidding? She probably has an entire drawerful by now. Set up an abortion fund instead.

•

Q.   My son's eighteenth birthday is coming up and I want to give him a special present. What would be appropriate?

A.   The want ads.

•

Q.   Why is it religious Jews circumcise their children at birth?

A.   They're pleased that the kid is already getting twenty percent off. That's why most of the rest of us do it, too.

•

Q. What's the difference between a "debutante ball" and a "coming-out party"?

A. The latter includes faggots.

Weddings

You know how to stop a man from fucking, don't you? (Marry him.) So can you blame a woman for being so picky about her last whack at romance? As the groom, you have almost no social responsibilities except putting out on the wedding night, so let her indulge herself. After all, you're not paying—or if you are, you're making a big mistake. Ever heard of an "eligible bachelorette," except on the *Dating Game*? Ditch her and move on to someone hungrier.

The Engagement

Q. Our daughter has announced her plans to marry a pleasant enough young man. Are we expected to shell out for an engagement party as well as for the wedding itself?

A. If she is not pregnant and has succeeded in extracting a diamond ring from a solvent heterosexual, quit bitching.

Q. How much should a guy spend on a wedding ring?

A. More than he can afford.

•

Q. My fiancé has given me an engagement ring I can't stand. Can I say something, or must I grin and bear it?

A. Sell it and buy something nice—men never notice these things.

•

Q. How and when should I let my old boyfriend know of my engagement? I haven't told him we're through yet.

A. An invitation to the wedding should clue him in.

•

Q. My fiancée's family cannot afford a lavish wedding, but my parents think it's important and have volunteered to pay for the entire affair. If that's okay, does my mother have control of the plans?

A. Absolutely. Money talks.

•

Q. My daughter is getting married and I want to place an engagement announcement in the local paper, but I'm concerned people may find out that I divorced my husband because he's a homosexual. How should this be handled?

A. The announcement should read: "Mrs. Jane Doe announces the engagement of her daughter Joan Doe to Mr. John Smith. Miss Doe is also the daughter of Mr. Jim Doe, a faggot and pederast now residing in Trenton, New Jersey."

•

Q.   My future mother-in-law has presented me with a family heirloom for an engagement ring . . . which happens to be incredibly ugly. Do I have to accept it and wear it the rest of my life?

A.   No. Trying to get along with a mother-in-law is an exercise in futility.

•

Q.   I'm getting married in June and don't want to take my husband's surname. Do you think this will have embarrassing social repercussions?

A.   Depends on his last name. If it's Getty or Rockefeller, I'd keep it.

•

Q.   At my bachelor party my pals procured a real prostitute and gave me a lot of grief because I wasn't interested in her favors. Were they acting in good taste?

A.   They were; *you* weren't. Are you queer or something?

•

Q.   Is a bachelor party, complete with a prostitute, necessary?

A.   Yes, especially if your wife-to-be insists on sleeping alone the night before the wedding.

•

Q. As best man, it's my responsibility to arrange the bachelor party. Should I hire a prostitute for the groom?

A. Yes, if you think lessons will do him any good this late in the game.

•

Q. Would it be inappropriate to invite my mother to a stag party I'm throwing for my cousin?

A. Yes, but it should then be called a doe party—better yet, a doe-doe party.

•

Q. I'm a Sikh immigrant from Amritsar, India, and don't know that I can afford a proper American wedding for my daughter. Do you have any suggestions as to how to cut costs?

A. I don't want to hear it. Use the money you've saved on haircuts.

•

Q. I am engaged to a man for whom it will be a second marriage. Must this be mentioned in the wedding announcement?

A. Yes. If you want people to know you're settling for used goods.

Showers

Showers, I don't care if they're wedding, birth, or even divorce, are all wet. Hell, it's like the pre-pre-

game show. Next comes engagement parties, bachelor parties, bachelorette parties, and on and on. Give it a break. Don't be so fucking greedy. Next time you're invited to someone's shower, show up with a bar of soap and a towel.

If you don't agree, follow these helpful points so you can all make asses out of yourselves together.

COME TO A WEDDING SHOWER!
For: Muffy Lockjaw
Date: November 15
Place: 69 Chestnut Street, Apt. 2C
Time: 5:30 P.M.–7:30 P.M.

P.S. Please bring something for the kitchen.
Remember, Muffy loves plaids.
RSVP: Mindy Dogood
555-3752

Translated, the above invitation really says:

"My friend Muffy wants some presents NOW! No waiting till after the wedding, because by then she may want out. Not only must you bring a present, in this case for the kitchen, but I'm *not* serving anybody any dinner and you must leave by 7:30. Make sure you bring *me* a nice bottle of wine.

"Muffy, you owe me."

•

Q. My best friend is pregnant and getting married. What kind of shower should she have?

A. Showers come in three varieties: wedding, baby, and golden. In your friend's case you might combine all three: bring baby gear, lingerie or housewares, and then piss all over them.

•

Q. What's an appropriate gift to bring to a "Bed 'n Bath" wedding shower?

A. Rubber sheets. These are suitable for all three types of showers.

•

Q. When should a baby shower be held?

A. When someone is pregnant. (Jews wait until after the birth because they don't want to waste money if the baby's stillborn.)

•

Q. Are coed baby showers the norm now? My wife is all set on the idea but I'm not too enthusiastic about it.

A. The only coed showers I like involve soap and water.

•

Q. I threw a baby shower for a friend, but the baby died within a few hours of birth. What should I do about the gift I gave her?

A. Ask her to return it, or at least give you your money back.

•

Q. I just found out that some friends are throwing me a wedding shower and have spent a lot of money on gifts. Unfortunately, my fiancé and I broke up over the weekend. When do I break the news to them?

A. After the party.

•

Q.   Coed baby showers seem to be replacing the old-fashioned women-only type. What's the difference?

A.   At the latter, there's a lot less talk about heavy flow days, nipple hair, and panty shields.

•

Q.   Is it within current social bounds to throw a divorce shower?

A.   Yes. And it's so much easier to buy for one than for two.

•

Q.   I've never been so mortified in my life as I was at a friend's bridal shower. A number of the gifts were disgusting sex things: whips, handcuffs, crotchless panties, rubber sheets, and so on. I think it was beyond the pale of correct social behavior, don't you?

A.   Oooh, don't stop—you're making me wet.

Invitations

Q.   Should I reply to a formal wedding invitation?

A.   Only if it speaks to you first.

•

Q.   Two days ago I broke off my engagement, but the invitations have already been sent out and the wedding's in less than a week. What should I do?

A.   Panic.

•

Q. My husband and I have been invited to the wedding of an Italian couple. What should I wear?

A. Something red, purple, blue, orange, green, yellow . . .

•

Q. The groom's family are paying half the cost of the wedding and they wish their names included on the invitation. Also, my name's different from my daughter's because I've since remarried, and the groom's mother is divorced yet not remarried but she's dating a black man, and my former husband wants to bring along his secretary. How should the invitation read?

A. If the kids had any smarts, they'd elope.

•

Q. I'm a widow, marrying a widower. What kind of invitation should we send to friends and family?

A. How about: "The surviving half of the Smith family and the last living member of the Jones family request the pleasure of your company."

•

Q. Can I bring a date to a wedding that I know's going to be really boring?

A. The wedding or the date? If both are boring, stay home.

•

Q. My fiancée's family is not rich enough to pay for the formal wedding we want, so my parents have offered to foot the bill. What should we do, and how should the invitation read?

A. Accept your parents' offer and make sure her parents —and all the guests—know about it. Keep the in-laws' guest list to a minimum, and ignore any suggestions they may have. Cut costs by making her side of the family serve the food and drink. The invitation should read:

Mr. and Mrs. John Doe
invite you to the wedding of their fortunate daughter
Jane
to Bob Smith
whose parents are footing the entire bill
(insert time and place)

•

Q. I have just received a wedding invitation from a gay college friend. How should I handle the situation?

A. Give the happy couple a lifetime subscription to *Prevention* magazine.

The Bridal Party

Q. Can you give me some suggestions as to items I could wear on my wedding day to satisfy the old poem, "Something old, something new, something borrowed, something blue"?

A. Something old: see "something blue";
Something new: see "something blue";
Something borrowed: see "something blue";
Something blue: a friend's month-old dead baby. Strap it to your leg.

•

Q. Our daughter is pregnant but is insisting on having a large, formal wedding only weeks before the baby is due. Should she still wear a white dress?

A. Yes. It won't stain when her water breaks.

•

Q. Since white symbolizes purity, would it be in bad taste to wear it even though I'm not a virgin?

A. Of course not, you whore.

•

Q. My sister is marrying a man who used to be gay, and he has invited two of his more effeminate friends to be bridesmaids. How should this situation be handled?

A. Insist they shave their legs.

•

Q. I am not exactly a virgin, but still want to wear white at my wedding. Is this all right?

A. Is that like a little bit pregnant? Wear something not exactly white.

•

Q. My sister has selected a layered mauve chiffon dress for the bridesmaids, which makes us all look like unripe eggplants. Should we tell her how much we hate the dresses?

A. That's way too sensitive a subject. Instead tell her that you hate her fiancé and she should cancel the wedding.

•

Q. Is it true that all brides are beautiful? I'm hoping it'll be one less thing to worry about on my wedding day.

A. Nothing makes an ugly woman beautiful except a blind date—and I mean blind. As in without sight. As in the ability to see.

•

Q. I'm marrying a woman who works in my office. Which coworkers must we invite?

A. Only those people who are in a position to: (a) advance your career; or (b) give you an expensive wedding present. These usually coincide.

Service

Q. I have a bad stutter, which gets worse when I'm nervous. Is there any way to avoid saying the wedding vows aloud without shattering tradition?

A. N-n-n-n-nope.

•

Q. What fee should be paid to the minister who officiates at our wedding?

A. Cash is always tasteful, though you might see if he'll settle for sloppy seconds that evening.

•

Q.   My lover and I want to get married but our church refuses to perform the ceremony because we're gay. Do we have any recourse?

A.   Knock him up.

•

Q.   My lover and I are getting married next month. Since we are gay, we have a slight problem with the Episcopal service. At the end of the ceremony, the minister says, "You may kiss the bride." How should we handle this?

A.   Who's taller?

•

Q.   I'd prefer to have my mother accompany me down the aisle. Would this be inappropriate?

A.   Why not take her on the honeymoon, too? The groom would probably love a *ménage à trois* on the wedding night, assuming mom's not too dried up.

•

Q.   Instead of playing traditional music at the wedding, my fiancé and I would like to hear something more current such as "I Wanna Rock" by Twisted Sister. Is this an appropriate request to make to the church organist?

A.   No. "Stairway to Heaven" by Led Zepplin is much more ecumenical.

•

Q.   I am considerably taller than my fiancé and am afraid we will look silly standing together at the altar. Is there any solution besides his standing on a box?

A.   Not unless you want to kneel at his feet. Look at the bright side: you can rest your champagne glass on his head during the reception.

•

Q.   My daughter is insisting on a formal wedding even though she is visibly pregnant. Won't people laugh?

A.   You bet.

•

Q.   Although my dad's been confined to a wheelchair for six years, I still very much want him to escort me to the altar. However, I'm a bit concerned about how to carry it off without it looking odd. Any suggestions?

A.   Sit in his lap.

•

Q.   My fiancé dislikes wearing rings and refuses to wear a wedding band. Should I insist?

A.   Give him a choice: the wedding ring, or MARRIED tattooed to his forehead. Learn to be less rigid.

•

Q.   My fiancée is Jewish and I am Catholic. Where should the marriage be performed, and by whom?

A.   On stage with an MC officiating—with that combo, it's going to be a show.

•

Q.   I'm trying to economize where possible on my daughter's wedding. Must it really be a crystal glass that my future son-in-law breaks underfoot?

A.   Where I come from, we use glasses to drink out of.

•

Q.   I am marrying a lovely woman I met in my physical therapy class. As we are both confined to wheelchairs, do any special rules apply to the organization of the wedding?

A.   Don't spend a lot of money on the band, and discourage your bride from wearing a train.

•

Q.   At my niece's formal wedding I was quite surprised to hear the congregation break into cheers following the exchange of vows. Is this appropriate behavior in a house of prayer?

A.   Why not? Haven't you ever prayed at a ballgame?

Reception and Gifts

Q.   What's a nice present for two gay friends getting "married"? They're going through the ceremony and everything.

A.   How about a monogrammed pair of cock rings? If you spring for sterling silver, they can double as napkin rings.

•

Q. What should I say to people at the reception who ask why I am still unmarried?

A. Explain that your lesbian tendencies keep getting in the way.

•

Q. Is it absolutely necessary for the best man to toast the newlyweds? I loathe public speaking and have no idea what to say.

A. So mumble.

•

Q. Is it appropriate to offer congratulations to the bride?

A. Yes, if she's significantly taller or uglier than the groom.

•

Q. When should a wedding reception end?

A. When the booze is gone.

•

Q. I was invited to attend a wedding and reception but can't make either. Do I have to send a present anyway?

A. Fuck no!

•

Q. Where does the bridal party sit at the reception?

A. On their asses. Where else?

•

Q.   Is it tacky to display the wedding gifts at the reception which follows?

A.   No, but if you do, you must display everything, including the emotion lotion and fist-fucking vibrator.

•

Q.   My daughter wishes to hold her wedding reception at the family house. The problem is that she's marrying into a family of uncouth louts, and I'm worried about what they'll do to my lovely home.

A.   Hold the reception in the garage.

•

Q.   I hate to hand over another toaster or set of wineglasses, but I never know what's an appropriate gift for newlyweds. Any suggestions?

A.   An inflatable doll for him and a multi-speed dildo for her. They'll add years to their marriage.

•

Q.   How long after the wedding do you have to come up with a present?

A.   A year. Hold out, because most marriages don't last that long.

Divorces

Divorces can be as jolly as weddings, at least for the spectators, and you don't have to mind your manners nearly so much. Take sides, go for the spoils, enjoy.

———————

Q. I'm going through an ugly divorce and my soon-to-be-ex husband wants his ring back. I know it's been in his family for generations, but I feel that it's mine. What's the proper response to this sticky situation?

A. Sell it back to him. Add twenty-five percent for broker and handling charges.

•

Q. I realize that traditionally a divorcée retains her ex's last name, but I want to erase every trace of the creep. What can I do?

A. How about chopping his body up into small pieces?

•

Q. Does any protocol cover the division of family property following a divorce?

A. Yes. Darwinism: survival of the fittest.

•

Q. Should I invite my husband's ex-wife to our New Year's Eve party? I don't want to seem unfriendly.

A. As long as you're conspicuously younger and prettier, why not?

•

Q. My stepdaughter and I are the same size and often swap clothes. Is this in bad taste?

A. Not as long as dad doesn't get confused.

•

Q. Is it in bad taste to celebrate a long-awaited divorce with a party?

A. Yes, but why start behaving yourself at this point?

•

Q. How soon after my divorce is final may I announce my engagement?

A. Why wait? You've already fucked up once.

•

Q. My fiancé has been divorced three times, but is friends with all his ex's and would like them to attend our wedding. Where in the church should they be seated?

A. On his side of the aisle. Set a precedent by giving them the best seats, just in case you end up joining them.

•

Q. A good friend just announced his decision to divorce his wife. What should my response be?

A. "Let's fuck!"

•

Q. I've just told my jive-ass husband to get his black ass out of my house. Do I have to return the wedding ring?

A. I didn't know you people got married.

•

Q. My husband and my best friend don't know that I know they're having an affair. Is it appropriate for me to confront them and demand a divorce?

A. You'll have more fun if you casually let drop to your husband the fact that your best friend just contracted herpes simplex.

Holidays and Family Functions

" 'Tis the season to be jolly...." Bullshit. Holidays are nothing but a poor excuse for a vacation—and who wants to vacation with their in-laws? Why do you think so many people commit suicide over the Christmas holidays?

Since these family free-for-alls bring out the absolute worst in everyone involved, a little etiquette could save your life. Think of it as a tool to help you find out who spent more on whom, whether your cousin's really bringing that Jewish boy home for Christmas, and who's cooking what before you decide which invitation to accept.

Try out these tips during the next year's round of time-wasting festivities. And if they don't work, you can always adopt my policy: unless the particular event features a short, fat faggot in a wheelchair to make fun of, stay home.

Valentine's Day

Q. What kind of Valentine's gift is nice to share with friends?

A. V.D.

•

Q. Valentine's Day at the office is always a bit depressing —all the cute young secretaries get lots of goodies and we older women are left empty-handed. Is there any way to address this unfair situation?

A. Let it be known that you're available for sexual favors during coffee breaks and watch your In box fill up.

•

Q. I received a Valentine's Day card from a girl I can't stand. Should I tell her how I feel or continue to leave her in the dark?

A. Lead her on and see what you get for Christmas.

Easter

Q. My husband insists on driving us home from Easter dinner at his mother's, which is always a long and alcoholic affair. Would it be impolite to explain to my mother-in-law that these conditions are too dangerous to permit us to continue to attend?

A. Yes, it would be. Let Jesus be your copilot.

•

Q. My son married a shiksa, and their children don't know Yom Kippur from Halloween or Elijah from Santa Claus. How can I teach them the old ways?

A. Who the hell's Elijah?

•

Q. My son has been invited to the White House for the annual Easter Egg Hunt. Is there any special White House protocol?

A. Yes. No bending over if any congressmen are around.

Christmas

Q. Isn't it tacky to hang Christmas cards on a string all over the house?

A. Why not? Christ was hung up on a cross.

•

Q. I explained to my ten-year-old, Jessica, that "Oh, gross" was not a tactful response to Christmas presents she doesn't like. How do I handle this basic aspect of good manners?

A. Explain that faking it is a useful social skill—especially for girls—and that someday it will make her very popular. After all, isn't it how you got daddy to marry you?

•

Q. If you spent a great deal more on a friend's Christmas gift than he spent on you, should this fact be pointed out?

A. Hell, yes!

•

Q. Is it polite to send a Christmas card to someone in mourning?

A. In mourning, in evening—depends on when the mail's picked up.

•

Q. My slimy cousin always muscles me under the mistletoe and tries to French me. Do I have to go along with this crap just because it's Christmas?

A. No way—knee him in the Yule log.

•

Q. Is it okay to exchange a Christmas present for something you like better?

A. Sure, and it's easier than trying to dig the original gift up whenever the person drops by.

•

Q. I'm sure my no-good son-in-law cashes in all our nice Christmas gifts and spends the money on pot. How can I prevent this happening with future gifts?

A. Monogram them.

•

Q. I'm a thirty-five-year-old woman who still has trouble expressing pleasure over a Christmas gift. I know this is immature of me and hurts people's feelings, but I don't know how to go about simulating an enthusiastic response.

A. I bet you can fake orgasms, so why not Christmas cheer?

•

Q. Christmas should be a time of joy, but I find it the most depressing day of the year. I know it's not fair to wallow in my black mood while those around me are happy. Do you have any suggestions as to how I can pretend joy?

A. Don't bother. Everyone else is faking it too.

•

Q. Every year we send Christmas cards to all our friends. Unfortunately, my husband will spend this holiday in the hospital, where he's receiving cobalt treatment and chemotherapy for advanced stomach cancer. Since Christmas is a time of joy, should I let faraway friends know of his condition or just not mention it?

A. Make up cards with a photo of the family gathered around his hospital bed. Label the bald, skinny guy "Dad."

•

Q. How can I let people know I spent a lot of money on their Christmas gifts without coming right out and saying it?

A. Leave the price tag on "by accident," or "forget" to remove the charge slip from the shopping bag.

•

Q. Every year I'm sickened by the waste as our family exchanges tons of needless, extravagant gifts. Wouldn't it be appropriate for us all to donate gifts to a charity next Christmas?

A.   No! Where's your Christmas spirit?

•

Q.   At our house the Christmas spirit seems to evaporate as soon as the kids get their toys open and start fighting over who got the best or the most. How can we impress on them the importance of good manners and a generous attitude?

A.   Next Christmas don't give them anything.

Channukah

Q.   Why do the Jews celebrate eight days of Channukah while we Christians only have one day at Christmas?

A.   Moses was a better negotiator.

•

Q.   Why do Jews get all the holidays? Rosh Hashanah, Yom Kippur, eight days for Channukah—I'm sick of it! My boss is Jewish but I'll bet he doesn't know the difference between a yarmulke and a beanie. Do us non-Jews have any redress?

A.   Give 'em a break. They're just making up for all those weekends in the concentration camps when they had to work.

•

Q.   My boyfriend has invited me to his mother's house for dinner on the first day of Channukah and I want to be on my best behavior. Should I bring a Christmas present, or is there such a thing as a Channukah gift?

A.   Make it a Channukah gift. That way, if she doesn't like it you get seven more tries.

Thanksgiving

Q.   Must I serve a turkey at Thanksgiving dinner?

A.   No. Only invite people you like.

•

Q.   I hate to offend holiday cooks, but I also don't want to gain twenty pounds between Thanksgiving and New Year's. What's the answer?

A.   Bulimia.

•

Q.   Thanksgiving dinner at my sister's was fine until she started taking some fancy cooking classes. Last year it was a mess of bony little birds, and this year she tried to serve fish! How can we get her back to turkey 'n chitlins?

A.   Sho enuf! Show up with some Kentucky Fried Chicken, y'all.

•

Q.   I can't stand the hypocrisy of the Thanksgiving holiday. Everyone hugs and kisses but can't wait till the front door's closed to start gossiping and back-stabbing. I don't see where "good manners" enter into all of this double-talk.

A.   They don't. It took you this long to figure it out?

•

Q.   Whenever our family congregates for Thanksgiving, we end up fighting among each other. How can we avoid this in the future?

A.   Don't get together, you dummy.

Halloween

Q.   When neighborhood kids come trick-or-treating, should I let on that I recognize them, or pretend I don't know them and act scared?

A.   Act scared, especially if they're black, because they'll probably want more than just candy.

•

Q.   It's terrible to see the neighborhood children ruining their teeth and appetites with unhealthful candy at Halloween. Must I give it out?

A.   Hand out tofu and sesame snacks—and stand back from your windows.

•

Q.   For years my wife and I have held a huge Halloween costume party. We're beginning to tire of it, but we feel a sort of obligation to our guests to continue the tradition. Should we?

A.   You must be WASPs.

New Year's Eve

Q. I think New Year's Eve brings out the absolute worst in people and should be abolished as a public holiday, but people call me a killjoy when I say so. What do you think?

A. You're not just a killjoy, you're an asshole.

•

Q. Is it all right to give strangers a New Year's Eve kiss at the stroke of midnight?

A. Go for broke—slip 'em the tongue and anything else you can get away with.

Fourth of July

Q. Every family get-together during the Fourth of July holiday seems to be an occasion for idiotic and unflattering group photographs. How can I gracefully evade these photo roundups?

A. Expose yourself.

Funerals

Funerals are tacky. Not to mention dull. Unless you look great in black, encourage ailing friends to opt for a simple cremation. If you simply must attend, arrive late, blow your nose loudly and frequently, and think of it as a chance to ride in a stretch limo. And keep your eyes open—funerals are great places to meet people who are so depressed they'll go to bed with anybody.

Q.   For those unable to attend, I would like to record my father's funeral on videotape. Some members of the family feel this would be in questionable taste. What do you think?

A.   Go for it, but keep the deceased's costume changes to a minimum.

Q.   Friends have just told me of the death of my ex-husband, whom I divorced with much bitterness ten years ago. Should I attend the funeral anyhow?

A. Only if you're still single and you think there might be someone available among the living. Wear something bright and low-cut, and try not to laugh out loud.

•

Q. Is it acceptable to let mourners know of a personal cause to which contributions may be made in memory of the deceased?

A. Definitely, but instead of calling it the Arctic Fox Coat for the Bereaved Wife Fund, call it the Endangered Species Endowment.

•

Q. When should the will be read?

A. Before the person in question dies, so you know where you stand.

•

Q. Should one wear black to a funeral? What about a hat?

A. Hat, shoes, shirt, even pants. Go crazy.

•

Q. My husband's dying wish was to be buried in drag. I am miserable about his little secret getting out to the world. Must I obey his wishes?

A. Pretend it's your idea. One thing funerals are short on is laughs.

•

Q.   If the deceased has opted for cremation, is a memorial service held instead of a funeral?

A.   Yes. Bring plenty of marshmallows and maybe a frozen pizza or two.

•

Q.   How long after the funeral should I wait before asking the widow out?

A.   The days preceding and immediately following the funeral are when she'll need comfort and support. And one of the things depressing her the most is sure to be the prospect of never getting laid again. Cheer her up, go muff-diving.

•

Q.   How long must I pretend to be in mourning for my wife? I'd been waiting for fifteen years for the old bitch to kick the bucket.

A.   Let the "mourning" work to your advantage. Women love it when men cry—it brings out their maternal instincts, and usually their tits.

•

Q.   When is it appropriate to leave the coffin open for "viewing"?

A.   Not if the deceased died of strangulation or by going through the windshield.

•

Q.   Should I bring my nine-year-old son to his grandmother's funeral?

A. Only if he has been properly indoctrinated. Strangle a family pet or stray kitten and leave it out in the sun for a few days. Then explain to him that this is what's happening to Grandma and what will happen to him if he makes *one sound* inside the church.

•

Q. What type of food should I serve at the reception after the funeral?

A. Don't knock yourself out fixing fancy stuff; you can't compete with a stiff.

•

Q. How should a newspaper death notice be composed if the person who passed away committed suicide?

A. "Doe, John Karl, after a long depression; on December 25, 1984, whining, weak-willed husband of Jane Smith (use maiden name) and father of Bootsie, Moppsie, and Biff. Funeral at St. Steven's Church, 49th and Madison Avenue, at 11 A.M. Wednesday, January 1. Party to follow."

•

Q. I am an Afro-American with quite dark skin. Must I wear all black at my husband's funeral?

A. Yes. But to keep people from mistaking you for a shadow, smile a lot.

•

Q. When must I notify friends of a death in the family?

A. Before the smell does.

●

Q. What is the appropriate number of pallbearers for an Afro-American funeral?

A. Nine. Four for the coffin and five to carry the radio.

●

Q. My late father had many influential friends in the Polish community. How many should I ask to be pallbearers?

A. There're only two handles on a garbage can.

●

Q. What kind of music should I select for my husband's funeral?

A. Something lively. These affairs are usually frightfully dull.

●

Q. Is the immediate family of the deceased supposed to notify others as to where the funeral will be held?

A. No, but hints are all right. Give a door prize to those who figure it out.

●

Q. Is it permissible to have the funeral service at home?

A. Yes, if your backyard is large enough. I hear corpses make great fertilizer.

●

Q. My husband of thirty years just passed away. What should I do about my wedding ring?

A. Pawn it.

•

Q. According to most etiquette books, I must wear only black for at least one year following the death of my husband. Is it permissible to find someone to console me in the meantime?

A. Only if you stick with the color theme; go find yourself a Negro.

•

Q. When is a memorial service held instead of a funeral?

A. When they can't find the body.

•

Q. My husband left instructions for an elaborate funeral in his will—and not enough money to cover the costs. What should I do?

A. Borrow a barbecue and cremate the cheapskate.

•

Q. My great-aunt wants her beloved dachshund buried in a fancy pet cemetery. Not only will this involve an ongoing expense for the family, it seems to me to be in the poorest of taste. Must we indulge her?

A. Kill two birds with one stone. Buy a plot big enough for pooch and auntie.

PART II

Around the House

Etiquette around the house is important. Don't ask me why. My home is my castle and if you're lucky enough to be invited over, you play by my rules.

Of course, most of you don't subscribe to this philosophy. You're busy worrying about what to serve those people you don't like but owe a meal to. Are the beds made? Should I use toilet paper or a Kleenex tissue when I masturbate? Do anorexics eat leftovers? And who's going to clean up this mess? That's why this chapter starts with *Domestic Help.* If you can't afford servants, the remainder of the chapter is for you—you peon.

Domestic Help

Take this simple quiz.
I would rather give up: (a) my child for adoption; or
(b) the person who cleans my house.

If you selected (a), you've got the right attitude.
Alas, the good old days of an acknowledged servant class that could be treated like dirt are long
gone. So if you've found someone who'll clean the
toilets and not steal you blind, hang on to her at
all costs. After all, if she leaves, who else will you
feel superior to? Unless, of course, you've latched
onto one of those wonderful illegal aliens. If they
give you any shit, you can always threaten to deport them. Refuse to pay them minimum wage,
make them sleep in the garage, feed them scraps—
enjoy.

———

Q. What's the best way to confront a maid that you
think steals?

A. Fire her. What's she going to do, sue?

•

46

Q. Our cook is gay. Is that grounds for dismissal?

A. If there were no gay cooks, we'd all starve to death. Just check out his kitchen-AIDS.

•

Q. I think our nanny is fondling our four-year-old son's private parts. Should I confront her?

A. Only if you want to start bathing the little brat yourself. It's tough to get good help.

•

Q. What should I feed the hired help serving a dinner party?

A. Scraps.

•

Q. My husband's got eyes for our Puerto Rican maid. How can I tactfully address the situation?

A. Hire a hunky black chauffeur.

•

Q. My wife says the houseboy I hired is fine, but that he "doesn't clean like a woman." What can I do?

A. Compromise: hire a fag.

•

Q. We'll soon be in the market for a nanny. Our neighbor has a wonderful, cheerful Jamaican woman and I'd love someone just like her. What should I say?

A. Something like: "Are there any more at home like you?" or "How much are they paying you?"

•

Q. I was shocked to come home and find that our housekeeper had enlisted our five-year-old to help with the dusting and cleaning. What should I do?

A. Fire the maid, idiot.

•

Q. I've just hired my first housekeeper. Do I give her instructions or just see how she operates?

A. Twenty years ago you could have ordered her around. Today just pray she shows up.

•

Q. My wife cleans the house *before* the weekly maid arrives because she's embarrassed by the disorder. How can I make her understand that this is not necessary when dealing with hired help?

A. Put her to work on your car, or the lawn.

•

Q. I gave my maid's name to a friend. Now she's offered her more money, and I'm furious. Isn't this a real breach of etiquette?

A. Yes. A good maid is far more valuable than a good friend. Threaten to turn your maid in to Immigration.

•

Q. I'm sure it's silly of me, but although most domestic help in my town is black, I feel awkward ordering a colored person around. Should I?

A. No. It's in their blood, like dancing.

•

Q. I could cook and clean blindfolded better than our ancient maid, but we've had her so long I hate to fire her. What's the proper solution?

A. What are you, a charity? Give her cab fare and one of your old winter coats, and show her the door.

•

Q. Our Vietnamese housekeeper sometimes has difficulty with simple English phrases such as "The oven needs cleaning," but doesn't miss a twist in *Dallas* or *Dynasty*. Is there a tactful way to address this discrepancy?

A. Try, "No cleanee oven, no watchee TV."

•

Q. Once a week we have a maid come in to clean the house. Should I prepare lunch for her if I'm home?

A. Experiment on some fancy dish which uses up lots of pots and pans. Make her clean up. Don't pay her by the hour.

•

Q. If an inexperienced servant blunders when serving guests, should I correct him or her in front of the company?

A. No. Speak to the offender gently until the guests have left, then beat him or her senseless with a whip or cane.

•

Q. Our new housekeeper does the laundry, but I can't help feeling that it's a bit ill-bred to give her my intimate apparel to wash. Am I being oversensitive?

A. You think they're going to clean themselves? Don't be a jackass.

•

Q. My husband's new position entitles him to a car and driver, which is a new experience for me. How should I address the chauffeur?

A. Any way you want.

•

Q. My friends are constantly boasting about how many servants they have and how much they pay them. Isn't this vulgar practice in the poorest of taste?

A. Only if you don't have any.

Entertaining

Having people over to your home comes in a very poor second to eating out and is only recommended if you have servants. It's no fun wrestling with such issues as how to integrate a homosexual couple into your carefully planned seating arrangement, or how many Negroes is enough but not too many. If you get tricked into having a party, remember, it's your house. Serve the guests liver, make them play charades and sit on uncomfortable chairs, make fun of what they're wearing, and so on. The worst thing they can do is leave—and isn't that what you really want them to do anyway?

Cocktails

Q. If the topic at a cocktail party turns to one that is personally embarrassing, what should I do?

A. Quickly change the subject to a common friend's impotence or flat-chestedness.

•

Q. What should I do if someone I'm conversing with has the bad manners to gaze about the room instead of focusing on me?

A. Smack 'em, but first make sure they're not blind. If they're blind, smack 'em anyway; how are they going to know who did it?

•

Q. When olives are served as an hors d'oeuvre, what is the proper way to dispose of the pits?

A. Arrange them in a decorative pattern on the coffee table.
    Stuff them between the cushions of the couch.
    Put them up your nose.
    Bury them under the lettuce leaves.
    Feed them to the baby.
    Offer them to a farsighted guest.

•

Q. When is the correct time to invite someone over for cocktails?

A. Whenever you're thirsty or lonely or bored or need a drink.

•

Q. During a cocktail party, two of my guests started arguing. The pitch got so heated they practically came to blows. How should the host or hostess respond to this embarrassing situation?

A. Take bets from the other guests.
    Caution: If the combatants are both gay, hose them

down immediately. One minute you're an innocent by-stander, the next you're under arrest. Your guests will never forgive you.

•

Q. Is the bathroom the place to dispense cocaine?

A. Yes, it's the only door you can lock without raising suspicion.

•

Q. When should I bring out the cocaine at a cocktail party?

A. When the last guest has left—it's too expensive to share.

•

Q. When snorting cocaine, should I use a straw or a spoon?

A. A straw if it's yours, a tablespoon if it's someone else's.

Formal Entertaining

Q. I loved "theme parties" as a child and am wondering if they are correct for adults.

A. Here are some socially acceptable themes for the '80s:
—a Mortgage Party: Send your guests a bill and they get a year at eighteen percent to pay it off;
—an Androgyny Party: Everyone comes in drag and gets bummed out when they can't tell whom to pick up;

—a Baby Party: Nobody comes because they can't find baby-sitters.

•

Q. How can I politely tell dinner guests that putting one's elbows on the table is a deplorable habit?

A. Don't wait so long between courses, asshole.

•

Q. If you're not supposed to put your elbow on the table during a meal, what do you do with the other hand?

A. Put it in your lap. That way you can play with yourself—or your neighbor.

•

Q. What can be done to break up those awkward silences that often come over a dinner table? As a guest I feel ill at ease, and as a hostess I feel mortified.

A. Make up your mind: Are you the guest or the hostess? I can see how there'd be awkward silences with a schizo at the table.

•

Q. I never know what to serve at a dinner party because most of my friends are such picky eaters. How can I satisfy everyone's taste?

A. Why not create a theme meal, such as Polish Solidarity Night, with a menu composed of Spam, olive loaf, and Kraft processed cheese. Or try a Black Power Dinner: heroin and watermelon. My favorite is the Ethiopian Drought Diet, consisting of rocks on-the-rocks.

•

Q. Is it proper to lift a cheek when farting at a dinner party?

A. Only if you are sitting down, in which case the gesture serves to politely warn the person seated next to you.

•

Q. Our Chinese friends had us to dinner and served monkey brains—a great delicacy. We'd like to reciprocate and have them for an American supper. What should we serve?

A. Hot dogs and baked beans. It's all-American, and they'll be reminded of their meal long after they've left.

•

Q. What's the best way to cope with a drunk who passes out at the table during a formal dinner party?

A. Undress him and arrange him in compromising positions with a house pet (borrow a neighbor's if necessary). Take Polaroids.

•

Q. How should one react to guests who bring their unwanted children to a dinner party?

A. If the children are old enough, they're an excellent source of cheap labor.

•

Q. Where should I seat a guest who always smells like crusty old gym socks?

A. In between a farter and a bleeder. The person with terminal flatulence will think he's the one who stinks, and the woman having her period will be preoccupied with whether she's leaking onto the upholstery.

●

Q. Must I provide a "date" for a single woman friend I'd like to invite to a dinner party?

A. Not unless you plan to collect a stud fee.

●

Q. How late is "fashionably late"?

A. No more than half an hour, unless you're Polish and too dumb to read a watch or Mexican and too lazy to steal one.

●

Q. What can a host or hostess do about the silent dinner guest who makes no effort to contribute to the party?

A. During the cocktail hour, surreptitiously tape a sign on the offender's back which says something amusing like KICK ME, I LIKE COCK, or MY BRA IS PADDED. Your other guests will take over from there.

●

Q. Should I be offended if my dinner guests leave food on their plates?

A. Can't you cook?

●

Q. Is it important to have a balanced number of men and women at the dinner table?

A. Don't you know why guests are seated male/female, male/female? So faggots don't try to jerk each other off during the dessert.

•

Q. Does one serve red or white wine with beef?

A. Coordinate the wine with what you're wearing, not what's being served.

•

Q. How do I stop a dinner guest from launching off on the vivid details of a nasty hemorrhoid operation?

A. Quickly reach for the latest copy of *Truly Tasteless Jokes* (volumes I through VI available at your local bookstore), or counter with a story about popping your boyfriend's zits.

•

Q. What should I say to a guest who brings a bottle of wine to dinner—and asks for it back when he leaves?

A. Ask for your dinner back.

•

Q. Should I instruct an inexperienced dinner guest in how to eat an artichoke?

A. No. Let your guest entertain you.

•

Q.   We're having the UN representative from Poland and his wife over for dinner. Is there any special way to prepare?

A.   Label the silverware.

•

Q.   Today more and more people are smoking marijuana socially instead of drinking alcohol. Should I offer pot at my next dinner party?

A.   Yes, especially if you're a mediocre cook. The munchies make even the worst food palatable.

•

Q.   I've heard of formal European table service, the less formal American service, and the informal hostess-alone service. What is the North African table service?

A.   Just like the informal hostess-alone service, minus the food.

•

Q.   What should one do if far fewer people respond to a party invitation than expected?

A.   If it's not your party, take the hint and leave. If it is, kill yourself.

•

Q.   Is it impolite to ask guests to take their shoes off at the door?

A.   No, but you'd better be serving gook food.

•

Q. At a ball, where does the hostess usually receive?

A. That depends on who wins the coin toss.

•

Q. I'd like to invite two friends to a party I'm having, but they detest each other. How should I handle this sticky situation?

A. Invite both, and cancel any entertainment you may have had planned.

•

Q. When is it correct to state the time span of a party on the invitation?

A. When you want the boring people to leave early so you can get high with your friends.

•

Q. Is it more refined to serve coffee in a cup than a mug?

A. If you mean "Do you have to wash more dishes?" then the answer is yes.

•

Q. Is it impolite to bring up religion or politics in social conversation?

A. Yes. So tell a truly tasteless joke or two. (Volumes I through VI are available at your local bookstore.)

•

Q. May a guest who happens to be a professional entertainer be asked by the hostess to perform after dinner?

A. Ask before dinner. It's a better incentive.

•

Q. I play piano professionally, yet friends seem to think nothing of requesting a little background music—gratis, of course—at their parties. What should I say to them?

A. Something about union scale.

Everything Else

Q. I want to have a couple of swinging couples over to see some porno movies. What kind of food should I serve?

A. Anything cooked with Mazola or Crisco.

•

Q. How many times can you go to dinner at someone's house before you have to reciprocate?

A. If they're not counting, why should you?

•

Q. Is it okay to clean up the kitchen between the main course and the dessert?

A. Yes, if you're eating alone or if you're anal.

•

Q. I'm having my mother-in-law for dinner along with the rest of my husband's family. They're all picky eaters and she keeps a kosher kitchen. What should I make for dinner?

A. Reservations.

•

Q. We've invited our new neighbors, who just arrived from Ireland, over for a get-acquainted meal. What should we serve?

A. How about a six-pack and a potato?

•

Q. My husband loves to show up with an unannounced dinner guest every now and then, and I've been caught with not enough food. How should I handle this embarrassing situation?

A. Give the guest your husband's portion.

•

Q. A number of close friends who are gay are coming over to my house for brunch, but I don't think I have enough stools to accommodate everyone. Would it be tacky to use pillows?

A. Yes. Instead, turn the stools upside down.

•

Q. I'd like to invite the new child on the block to my six-year-old's birthday party (he's blind). How can I make sure he'll be entertained?

A. Suggest Hide 'n Seek—he's It. Or Monkey in the Middle—he's the Monkey.

•

Q. My children are taught not to swear or curse at the table, but last night Jimmy had a little black friend over

to dinner whose every word was either the F word or *shit.*
Should I have disciplined him?

A.   Fuck no; he was probably armed.

•

Q.   I'm thirteen years old and I want to have a coed
party. What kind of refreshments should I serve?

A.   Between your mom's medicine chest and your dad's
liquor cabinet, you should be fine. Have plenty of breath
mints on hand.

•

Q.   What do I say to friends who ask if they can bring
friends or houseguests to a party of mine?

A.   Give permission only if the friends' friends are members of minority races who will look good in white coats
and aprons.

Bed and Bath

No, I'm not talking about those cutesy little inns run by some organic family in Vermont. I'm referring to those inner sanctums of domestic privacy and sexual abandon: the bedroom and the bathroom. Besides not changing the sheets after an evening of water sports or leaving the bathroom so foul you need a gas mask to enter, what etiquette applies? None. Masturbate, do drugs, examine your turds, dance around with your underwear on your head, take advantage of those bathroom-tile acoustics—it's all okay.

If you're the type who's still too uptight to pee in the shower or to be cool when you fart in your partner's face during oral sex, here are some guidelines. You WASPs are going to love this chapter.

―――――――

First of all, how horny are you? (Score twenty-five points for each "True" answer.)

MALE

1. You don't read *any* of the words in *Playboy*.
2. Your palm is sore.

3. Your dog has a headache.
4. You'd fuck a duck.
5. You'd fuck a baby duck.
6. You'd fuck a baby duck with AIDS.

FEMALE

1. You put on a garter belt before going down to check your mail.
2. You're shopping twice a day for batteries for the vibrator.
3. You begin to think that lesbians are into a good thing.
4. You don't care if he has herpes.
5. You don't care if he has herpes and AIDS.
6. You don't care if he's dead, just stiff.

If you score more than fifty points, forget about etiquette. Get laid. Rape someone—an elderly woman or someone in traction if it'll take less time. Women, spread your legs for anyone, even the retarded kid next door. Better this than become a violent sex offender (unless you already are one).

Now you're ready to pay attention to the finer points of bedroom etiquette—read on.

Bedroom

Q. My husband likes to do it doggie style, but I find it very unromantic. Would it be rude to mention my feelings?

A. Bark whenever he mounts you. If he doesn't get the hint, start sniffing his balls in public.

•

Q. My girlfriend insists on using her vibrator when we make love. I find it a bit weird. Is this proper sexual behavior?

A. Yes, as long as she doesn't call it by name.

●

Q. When is the correct time to wear crotchless underwear?

A. During your period, for convenient tampon insertion. They don't have to be washed as often, either.

●

Q. What is the correct response to someone who sneezes while performing cunnilingus?

A. Squeeze harder, especially if he hits that magic G-spot. Otherwise a simple "God bless you" will suffice.

●

Q. If you don't want to swallow, is it okay to spit it out in the ashtray?

A. I hate sticky ashtrays! Use the floor like the rest of us.

●

Q. My husband is turned on by my used sanitary napkins. Is this perverted?

A. It's cheaper than leather or lingerie. Store them for him in Zip-loc bags in the freezer to keep them fresh and fragrant between cycles.

●

Q. Is it proper to have sex for the first time with someone if I happen to have my period?

A. Not unless your partner is a vampire or a hemophiliac.

•

Q. Is oral sex fattening? My girlfriend says going down on me ruins her diet.

A. Only if your cock is lubricated with peanut butter, as, of course, it should be at all times.

•

Q. I am mortified by the sounds that sometimes occur when air is trapped inside the vagina during intercourse. Is there a tactful way to cover up for these embarrassing moments?

A. Tell him you're a ventriloquist.

•

Q. I think my roommate is gay. I don't want to accuse him and make him feel uncomfortable, but is there a polite way of finding out?

A. See if his cock tastes like shit.

•

Q. My wife is on the plump side, which doesn't bother me, but she's very self-conscious about it. She gets particularly upset when we make love and I have trouble locating her vagina. Is there a tactful way to address this problem without upsetting her?

A. No. Just roll her in flour and go for the wet spot.

•

Q. My girlfriend keeps misplacing her diaphragm and at times it is very awkward. Should I tell her how rude this behavior is?

A. No, silly! Pin it up on the wall over her bed instead.

•

Q. A good friend has decided to "come out" as a homosexual. We're delighted he's joining our group and want to give him a present. Do you have any suggestions?

A. AIDS.

•

Q. After making love, should I offer to clean up my partner's private parts?

A. Sure, douche bag.

•

Q. Where's the best place to insert your diaphragm, in the bathroom or the bedroom?

A. Try between your legs, idiot.

•

Q. The walls in my building are thin and the ceaseless sexual activity of the couple next door is audible day and night. May I ask them to keep the noise down?

A. Hell no. It's cheaper than cable TV.

•

Q.   My downstairs neighbor plays disco music day in and day out; he even leaves the station on while he's at work. It drives me nuts, and he ignores my requests that he turn it down. What's the solution?

A.   Move to a white neighborhood.

Bathroom

Q.   Is it appropriate to keep birth-control pills in the medicine cabinet?

A.   Sure, if you want everybody who comes over to know you fuck with chemicals.

●

Q.   Some of my friends have admitted they urinate in the shower. Isn't this disgusting?

A.   No, but taking a dump is something else again.

●

Q.   Last week I asked to use the toilet at some friends' house. Much to my chagrin, when I finished, I noticed they'd run out of toilet paper. What should I have done?

A.   Drip dry.

●

Q.   When visiting the hostess' bathroom, is it all right to "borrow" some of her expensive perfume to freshen up a bit?

A.   Sure, and why not pocket some of her jewelry, rip off her silverware, and rifle through her closet too.

•

Q. When is it appropriate to use condoms?

A. When she won't let you come in her mouth.

•

Q. When's the right time to put a condom on?

A. *After* you've taken a leak.

Houseguests

Face it: it's not much fun being a houseguest *or a* host. The guest is supposed to be helpful without getting in the way, while the host has to deal with feeding an extra mouth, making beds, and being civil in the morning—all the while taking the terrible risk that the guest will be so comfortable he'll stay on. Why do you think God invented motels?

I recommend that no owner of a spare room or bed offer it to anyone outside his own family and that no visitor be exempt from kitchen or yard work. The questions in this section are from people too dumb to say, "No. Go away."

Q. What is the origin of the phrase, "Houseguests, like fish, stink after three days"?

A. The actual phrase is "After three days, women still stink like fish," and is self-explanatory. You may have been thinking of the old proverb: "Der houseguests bein der strudel scarfers." (Translation: "Houseguests suck.")

•

Q. My daughter is bringing her college boyfriend home for spring break. Should I prepare one room or two?

A. Why knock yourself out; they're going to fuck and suck no matter what. Make up one bed—you'll have less laundry.

•

Q. What is an appropriate gift for a weekend guest to bring?

A. Something perishable that must be consumed during the visit.

•

Q. My husband is very allergic—is it appropriate for me to ask weekend guests to leave their pedigreed Siamese cats at home?

A. Send your husband away for the weekend: cats are easier to care for.

•

Q. Should friends who spend the weekend be asked to help around the house?

A. Absolutely. It's the perfect time to clean out the filthy garage or tackle that mess in the attic. Set up a "chore board," and award points toward valuable prizes such as a meal or a place to sleep.

•

Q. If houseguests are making too much noise during sex, is it impolite to ask them to stop or at least to keep the grunting and groaning down?

A. Keep quiet. You may learn something.

•

Q. When visiting for the weekend, should I bring my own vibrator or ask our hostess if I might use hers?

A. Bring your own—hers may be in the shop for repairs.

•

Q. Two gay friends from work are planning to visit, and my eight-year-old is confused by the fact that they are sharing a room. How should I explain the social proprieties to him?

A. Explain that the two men will be practicing revolting sexual perversions under your roof, but that you have to let them because mommy's job depends on it.

•

Q. What should a guest say who has just spilled a large glass of red wine onto her host's new white shag rug?

A. "Oh, shit."

•

Q. Do I really have to change the sheets between each guest's visit?

A. Who's going to know? If they get too stiff and crusty, turn them over.

•

Q. Is it okay to check out your hostess's medicine cabinet?

A. How else are you going to find out if she has hemorrhoids or herpes?

•

Q. I've been asked to spend a weekend with friends who pride themselves on not allowing liquor in their house—but I look forward eagerly to the cocktail hour. What should I do?

A. Sounds to me like someone's afraid of the D.T.s. Reconsider the invitation over a drink.

•

Q. My husband and I spent a wretched weekend in the country as houseguests. Our room was next to that of the colicky baby, the mattress was lumpy, and the corners were full of spiders. How could we have departed early without embarrassing our hosts?

A. Why wouldn't you want to embarrass them?

•

Q. My son is bringing home his male lover for the weekend. Should I let them share the same room?

A. Yes. Leave a jar of K-Y Jelly on the bedside table so you can get some sleep.

•

Q. When guests wake up hungry before their host and hostess, what should they do?

A. Make a lot of noise.

•

Q.   We've been invited for the weekend by friends who have a lovely house—and a very spoiled child. Any suggestions?

A.   Wait until Sunday evening to swat the kid.

•

Q.   Is it polite to ask a weekend hostess whether you may do your laundry?

A.   If she's your mother.

•

Q.   A friend of mine married a Frenchwoman, and they frequently speak French to each other. Of course I can't understand what they're saying. Isn't this extremely rude?

A.   *Moi, je m'en fou.*

•

Q.   Whose responsibility is it to clean those pesky rings around the inside of the bathtub, the guest's or the host's?

A.   If you have been invited to spend the night, it's the host's problem. If you're only there for dinner, what the hell are you doing taking a bath?

Invalids

Sick people are not only unpleasant to be around, they may be contagious. This goes for psychos too. Nevertheless, until you're positive that you don't stand to inherit or that the brain damage is irreversible, those pesky sickbed visits are probably unavoidable. Take heart: there are usually some good drugs around to try and pocket. If these sick calls get on your nerves, remember: a bedridden person is a helpless person, so in the long run it doesn't really matter how you treat them.

———

Q. My girlfriend has a great body, and coincidentally she just loves to show off the scar from her recent gallbladder operation. Isn't this in bad taste?

A. Be glad she doesn't have any episiotomy scars.

•

Q. When they find out I'm a doctor, complete strangers think nothing of coming up to me at social gatherings and asking "just one question" about their latest symptom.

How can I get them to respect the fact that I'm not on the job?

A.   Tell them to undress. If they do, ask for a blow job.

•

Q.   A friend just returned from the hospital after a bout with throat cancer. The doctor had to remove my friend's larynx. Now he presses a vibrator against his neck to talk and he sounds like a machine. It creeps me out—how should I handle the situation?

A.   Ask him to do impressions of C3PO, HAL, or Robbie the Robot.

•

Q.   I have herpes. Should I tell my date before, during, or after we go out?

A.   If you want to get laid, keep your mouth shut.

•

Q.   What should I send a friend who's been diagnosed as having MS?

A.   The tapes of *Dance Fever* or *Disco Madness.*

•

Q.   I'm having a dinner party and have invited my seventy-year-old aunt. Unfortunately, she has Parkinson's disease and shakes constantly. She's very proud and would sooner spill food than ask for help. What should I do?

A.   Set the table with chopsticks and serve Jell-O.

•

Q. The kid next door has hemophilia. He's a real pain in the ass, but I can't slug him and he knows it. Do I really have to play with him?

A. No. If your mother makes you, play darts.

•

Q. My assistant has AIDS and is slowly dying in front of my eyes. What are my social responsibilities?

A. Stay away; it's a social disease.

•

Q. My mother-in-law is bedridden and recently moved in with us. Now I'm expected to wait on her hand and foot. How far do my responsibilities extend?

A. As far as her reach.

•

Q. I have AIDS, but from the way people treat me you'd think I have the plague. They won't even shake hands. Could you please point to your readers the insensitivity of this behavior?

A. Let me sterilize the envelope first.

•

Q. My husband, a physician, suffers from a neurological condition. His trembling in no way impairs his professional judgment but patients have been leaving his practice anyway. May I say something to them?

A. Face it—who wants a crip for a doctor?

•

Q. I don't think people understand how cruel they can be when joking about AIDS. Behavior like that goes beyond the proper social boundaries. Can you tell your readers something about this terrible illness so they can come to sympathize?

A. Sure. AIDS stands for Adios, Infected Dick-Sucker.

•

Q. A good friend has lost her sight and refuses to leave her house. I'm determined to cheer her up and get her out. What would be appropriate?

A. A blind date.

•

Q. I am a divorcée who has recently had a breast removed in a cancer operation. When is the right time to let a date know he's not eyeing the real thing?

A. He's going to be repelled, so do it after he's spent a lot of money on dinner.

•

Q. I have a date with an epileptic. Where should I take her so she won't feel self-conscious?

A. Dancing—someplace with those neat strobe lights.

•

Q. What's the best way to address a paranoid schizophrenic?

A. "Pssst . . . hey you! No, not you, the other one."

•

Q. What type of meal should I prepare for my anorexic girlfriend?

A. Something light and inexpensive.

•

Q. A diagnosed manic-depressive is coming over for cocktails. What do they usually drink? And do I need a prescription for it?

A. Thorazine on the rocks. And yes.

•

Q. My neighbor's son is severely retarded and drools constantly on the upholstery when he and his mother come to visit. Should I say anything to the mother?

A. Store the kid in a garbage bag until the visit's over.

PART III

Out and About

Unless you're a total xenophobe, you must occasionally leave the sanctuary of your homes and face weirdos in the supermarket and retards in line at the bank, fatties on blind dates and gropers at the health club. Contact with other humans is unavoidable.

"But, Blanche," you may protest, "I like being around other folks. They don't bother me as much as you think." People who talk like this are either used-car dealers or stockbrokers. Or, worst of all, nerdy authors of self-help books.

If we're such social animals, why are we the only living organisms that devote massive amounts of time and money to killing our own kind? Think about it. Okay, that's enough. Lighten up. Lock your door, unplug the phone, and read this section.

Dining Out

Restaurants

This chapter would be a lot shorter if people subscribed to Blanche's philosophy of eating out: money talks. As long as you can cover the tab, no other etiquette is required for a restaurant meal. You call the shots.

———

Q. Why do woman always go to the bathroom in groups while dining out at resturants?

A. To compare menstrual discharge. You had to ask.

•

Q. How many after-dinner mints is it polite to take?

A. As many as will fill your pockets and purse. You think they're going to call the cops or something?

•

Q. Must I tip a waiter who's been particularly rude?

A. Yes. A useful tip is, "Look both ways before crossing the street."

•

Q. I'm a young guy, and my poetry professor invited me to dinner and then someplace called The Crisco Disco. I'm really honored. Is there something I should bring?

A. A tube of K-Y Jelly.

•

Q. Many of my friends have dogs, which is fine, but I can't stand these animals jumping up on me every time I come over. What can I do to discourage this behavior?

A. Kick them in the crotch (either the pet's or the pet owner's, whoever's smaller).

•

Q. Is it okay to suck an orange in public?

A. It's a hell of a lot easier than sucking a black.

•

Q. When should I use a fork and when should I use my fingers while eating out at a fancy restaurant?

A. Use your fingers on anything too heavy for a fork.

•

Q. I was brought up to consider eating in public to be in bad taste. What do you think?

A. You must have a tough time at restaurants.

•

Q.   If you're out of Kleenex, is it okay to blow your nose on the linen napkin?

A.   Use the edge of the tablecloth; it'll dry out faster.

•

Q.   Many of the women I date earn as much money or more than I do, but I feel obliged to pick up the check. Should I?

A.   Sure; pick it up, then hand it over.

•

Q.   I hate spending a lot of money on a woman who's not going to put out. Is there a correct way to gauge how much one should spend?

A.   Depends on the quantity and quality of sexual services she's providing. Restrict her to pizzas and burgers or Dutch treat till she puts out. A good blow job is worth a movie and a Mexican meal. Special attention to anal sex, bondage, or any other quirks deserves a French or Continental splurge.

•

Q.   Is is impolite to eat the garnishes in your cocktail?

A.   Only Puerto Ricans and vacationing New Jerseyites order drinks with fruit salad in them.

•

Q.   Should a restaurant be expected to provide high-chairs and other amenities for the children of customers?

A. Yes, if "highchair" and "other amenities" are euphemisms for gags, restraints, and a shelf in the coat-check room.

•

Q. Is it okay to ask people at an adjoining table to refrain from smoking?

A. I don't give a shit. What do you think I am, your mother or something?

•

Q. I want to impress my new girlfriend with a classy meal, but I can't read those fancy French menus. Any suggestions?

A. Don't date women who read French.

•

Q. What's the best way to deal with those damn strolling musicians in a restaurant?

A. Put your hands over your ears and drum your feet on the floor until they veer off toward another table. If that fails, sing "My Way" at the top of your lungs.

•

Q. I'm usually too intimidated to complain about poor service in a restaurant. Are there any rules of thumb to go by?

A. If you're Puerto Rican, threaten the waiter with your switchblade. If you're Polish, you probably forgot what you ordered—so it doesn't matter if the waiter did, too. If you're a WASP, say nothing and leave a twenty percent tip.

•

Q.   When dining out with a group of friends, what's the proper way of splitting the check?

A.   Order the most expensive dishes on the menu and insist that the check be divided equally.

•

Q.   In three of the four restaurants I've eaten in lately, the waitress has stacked the dishes at the table. I find this behavior very rude; what do you think?

A.   That's nothing. I've woken up at a few bars where the waiters started stacking the patrons.

•

Q.   Whenever I go out to eat I feel obliged to leave a tip, even if the waiter or waitress was slow or rude. Must I?

A.   Yes. That will be five dollars, please, Bozo.

•

Q.   Recently I waited on a party of four blacks who ran up a tab of over $100 and left me a two-dollar tip. Should I have said something?

A.   Probably not. Blacks have trouble with numbers. Next time give them their bill in ounces or grams.

•

Q.   The other day I went to a restaurant for a nice quiet meal, only to be interrupted by a couple with a screaming infant seated next to me. Would it have been rude to say something to them about the noise?

A.   Something along the lines of "Shut that fucking kid up" usually works for me.

•

Q.   My father insists that my date should give her order to me and that I, in turn, should transmit it to the waiter. Isn't this kind of dumb?

A.   Yes, but useful if she is exceptionally stupid or a deaf mute.

•

Q.   I want to impress my date by ordering some fancy-schmancy wine. Can you suggest how one goes about this properly when restricted to a tight budget?

A.   Order anything with a screw top.

•

Q.   I like to think of myself as a guy with some savoir-faire, but those ten-page wine lists always confuse me. Do you have any tips so that I don't blow it in front of my date?

A.   She'll just be looking at the prices, so order something expensive.

•

Q.   I realize it's considered chic these days to dine at African-style restaurants, with everyone using their hands and eating from a common dish. Yecch! Is there any way to go along with this without catching some disease?

A.   Wear gloves.

•

Q. Is it all right to breast-feed in a restaurant?

A. Yes. And it comes in very handy when the waiter's late with the cream.

•

Q. What's the proper way to indicate the location of the ladies' room to a female dinner guest?

A. Stand up and point with your pecker.

•

Q. My husband is confined to a wheelchair, and on more than one occasion we have discovered that a restaurant's restroom was located down a treacherous flight of stairs. In a situation like this, should I try to maneuver him down the stairs and risk an accident, or request help from an able-bodied waiter?

A. One little shove and you get the old crip's insurance —not to mention the proceeds of a nice lawsuit. Then you can go out and get yourself a man who walks, talks, and fucks like a normal human being.

•

Q. If you can't swallow a piece of food at the dinner table, what's the best way to get rid of it?

A. Spit it out and demand that the chef identify it.

•

Q. Is there a proper way to eat spaghetti? I know that using a spoon is uncouth, but it's the only way that works for me.

A. Order ravioli.

•

Q. Do I really have to give a quarter to the attendant who hands out towels in the ladies' room?

A. Not if it's the only time you'll be going there.

•

Q. My wife and I had dinner at an expensive restaurant last week, but our meal was all but ruined by a group of loud and obnoxious people seated next to us. What should we have done?

A. Told them to "shut the fuck up."

•

Q. Is it all right to eat chicken with your fingers at a restaurant?

A. It's easier than using your toes.

•

Q. What do I do at a restaurant when served a dish I can't identify?

A. You ordered it, moron.

•

Q. My friends make fun of me for not using chopsticks when we go out to Chinese restaurants, but when I try to, I hardly get any food into my mouth. What should I do?

A. Shovel it in with your fork. Chopsticks are for gooks.

Dinner Parties

There may be no such thing as a free lunch, but plenty of people will invite you over for a free dinner. And since you're not being charged for the meal, you have nothing to lose. Fuck 'em if they can't take a joke.

Q.   At a formal diner is it okay to mop up gravy with your bread?

A.   A sponge is more absorbent.

•

Q.   We're often invited to a certain friend's house for dinner, and more times than not the silverware is filthy. Would it be offensive to wipe it off with a napkin, or should we just eat with it as it is?

A.   Wiping it off would be insulting. Bring your own.

•

Q.   As a dinner guest, I understand it's rude to leave food on your plate. What should I do if I can't possibly manage one more bite?

A.   Mail it to Ethiopia.

•

Q.   My fiancé has the disgusting habit of picking his nose when he thinks no one's looking and sticking the boogers under the table. What can I do?

A.   Tell him to bottle them and sell 'em as bacon bits.

•

Q. Should a lady wear gloves to a formal dinner?

A. Yes. They'll come in handy if she loses her napkin.

·

Q. I returned from a formal luncheon to find I had inadvertently pocketed one of the hostess's antique silver saltcellars. May I simply sneak it back, or must I return it with a proper note of apology?

A. What use is a saltcellar without a pepper mill? Go for the pair.

·

Q. What's the polite response when you're invited to a party on an evening when you have a prior engagement?

A. "Who's coming?" and "What're you serving?"

·

Q. Some wealthy friends have invited me to a party and hinted broadly that there's going to be plenty of "blow." Is there anything I need to know before trying cocaine for the first time?

A. DON'T sneeze.
    DON'T snort more than one line at a time unless no one is looking.
    DON'T say, "Gee, I forgot which end I put in my nose" when you pass the straw along.
    DON'T save your boogers for later.
    DO let me know where the party is.

·

Q. During a dinner party a week ago, I sat across from a woman who constantly picked her nose. What's worse is that she ate what she found. I almost threw up. Should I have said something?

A. It's not your role to play nose police unless it's your party. Tell her politely to save room for dessert.

•

Q. Is it rude to take the last hors d'oeuvre from the plate at a cocktail party? So often I see food wasted because no one wants to be seen taking it.

A. Go for it, piggy.

•

Q. We have some boring friends who keep inviting us over for dinner. How long can we keep putting them off?

A. And turn down a free meal?

•

Q. Energy-conscious friends (I think they're just cheap) keep their house in the fifties. What should we wear if we're invited over to dinner?

A. How about Sandra Dee socks and an Elvis Presley jacket?

•

Q. If a coaster isn't in sight, should I just put my glass down on the table?

A. Yes. It's not your fault the hostess fucked up.

•

Q. If I'm invited over to friends for dinner, should I volunteer to help clean the dishes after the meal?

A. Hell no. Hide out in the bathroom until the cleanup is complete.

•

Q. If my host fails to refill my wineglass after a suitable interval, should I say something?

A. Try, "Who do you have to fuck to get a drink around here?"

•

Q. I'm invited to a fondue party. Does any special etiquette apply?

A. Just the standard rules of fencing.

•

Q. Is it antisocial to sit down during a cocktail party? I get so tired standing all the time.

A. Not if you'd rather give blow jobs than talk.

•

Q. Is it impolite to read a magazine when you're trying to get through a boring party?

A. No. You're the guest. Listen to the radio, turn on the TV, enjoy yourself.

•

Q. How many cocktails can one drink without appearing to be a lush?

A. And what's wrong with being a lush?

•

Q. What should you do with your napkin after the meal is over?

A. Wipe your mouth, stupid.

The Office

We all know the basic premise behind success in the workplace: kiss your boss's ass and screw your coworkers, simultaneously if possible. Fortunately, the finer points of office etiquette exist to make your blind quest for power and money look legit.

Sure, there are etiquette books for goons which describe how to dress for success, what to say in interviews, and the proper way to answer the company phone. But how many tell you how to deal with a boss when she's on the rag, when a blow job might go further than a memo, how to get away with hiring only women with big tits, and the correct way to unload minority employees without losing valuable tax credits? Let Blanche show you the way to getting ahead without getting caught. After all, if you've got to work hard, play dirty.

Interviews

First, some tips on landing a job:

DO	DON'T
Show up for the interview whenever it's convenient.	Beg.
Relax. Kick off your shoes and loosen your tie or top buttons of your blouse.	Grovel.
Offer the interviewer a beer or joint to establish a good rapport.	Be obsequious.
Blame past job fuck-ups on others.	Fawn.
Give the interviewer shit if he keeps you waiting.	Whimper.

If the interview is ending and you haven't yet been offered a job, reverse the above procedure.

•

Q. Is it appropriate to point out a large booger hanging out of the interviewer's nose?

A. Yes, and point out small and medium-size boogers while you're at it.

•

Q. My boss wants me to interview his vacuum-brained daughter for a job in my department. How do I say no without jeopardizing my own position?

A. Why put your job on the line when you can risk someone else's? Make your assistant interview her.

•

Q. How should I follow up an interview?

A. With prayer.

•

Q. Is it common to be asked to take one's clothes off during an interview?

A. Yes, if you are being measured for a uniform or the air conditioning has broken down.

•

Q. What does it mean if an interviewer takes his pants off during the interview?

A. He wants to see how you handle a Dictaphone.

•

Q. One interviewer asked me my breast measurements. Is this normal?

A. Depends on the size of your jugs.

•

Q. Peoples they tell for me, "Jerzy, you must for to wear proper dress when you to interview go." For what is this "proper dress"? Won't for I to look silly wearing dress?

A. Don't worry—they'd never hire a dumb Pole like you anyway.

•

Q. Our company is instituting an Equal Opportunity drive, and my responsibility is to fill a number of middle-management positions with minorities. What kind of ads should I run?

A. For blacks: "Yo, mama—check it out one time. The Man's got a gig fo ya. We be cool."

For Hispanics: "Yo, mamasita—check it out uno tiempo. Trabajo. We don' fuck weet su cabeza."

For the handicapped: "If yu cn rd ths, yu cn gt a gd jb."

•

Q. Is it okay to tell "little white lies" about oneself during the interview?

A. As long as you're not caught. For example, DO brag about your sexual prowess; DON'T brag about the limo waiting downstairs.

•

Q. What's the best way to let a job candidate know you've hired someone else for the job?

A. Tell the truth: that black men make you nervous, that you can't bear women with fat ankles, that the thought of his little Porky Pig voice on the intercom day after day makes your skin crawl. Face it (they'd better): what do brains or experience have to do with landing a job?

•

Q. Is it rude to chew gum during an interview?

A. Not if you're interested in a career in manual labor.

•

Q. I'm a guy interviewing with a woman boss. Should I list hobbies on my resume, and if so, which?

A. Scuba-diving will look better than muff-diving, but the latter might get you the job.

•

Q.   What's the best way to make a prospective employer sit up and take notice of my resumé?

A.   Include it as part of a ransom note.

•

Q.   What's a good way to make your resumé stand out?

A.   Print it on $100 bills.

•

Q.   Is there any graceful way to avoid embarrassing people who show up for an interview at the incorrect time?

A.   Yes, but do you really want to waste good manners on somebody who can't tell time?

•

Q.   Is it necessary to ask permission first of someone you want to list as a reference?

A.   Yes, unless you don't care if they tell the truth.

Boss and Secretary

Q.   Just because I'm a secretary doesn't mean men can treat me like a thing. Please tell your readers that we should be treated with the same good manners as everyone else.

A.   You sound upset. Is it that time of month?

•

Q. When giving my boss a blow job, must I always crawl under his desk? I'm constantly straining my back and bumping my head against the inside desk drawer.

A. Your boss appears to have your best interests at heart. Wouldn't you be embarrassed if someone dropped in on him while you were giving head and saw you?

•

Q. Last week my superior praised me for a report I didn't write. Instead of correcting him, I thanked him. Now he wants to get rid of the person who actually wrote the report (my assistant) on the grounds that she's not carrying her share of the corporate workload. What should I do?

A. Not a thing. You can always get another assistant.

•

Q. I don't want to ruffle his feathers, but my boss is a terrible driver, and I'm afraid one of our sales calls is going to end in tragedy. Is there a diplomatic solution the next time this happens?

A. Bring up Chappaquiddick.

•

Q. Should I share my cocaine with my boss at the Christmas party?

A. Definitely not. Don't you know coke is God's way of telling people they're making too much money?

•

Q. My secretary is gorgeous and I can't get her out of my mind. I want her so badly it hurts. What should I do?

A. Fuck her. If she doesn't want to go along with it, threaten to fire her. Then fuck her.

•

Q. My secretary isn't very bright, but can she give a great blow job! How can I show my appreciation?

A. If you don't want to give her a raise every time she gives your dick a lift, change her title to something more lofty, such as "Head Secretary." A swell promotion.

•

Q. I call my secretary "my girl" and "my gal Friday," but she takes offense at these endearments. I think they're cute. Who's right?

A. See if she likes being called "my little dickwipe" any better.

•

Q. How do I convey to my boss that I'm a secretary, not a waitress? Every morning he asks me to go out and get him Danish and coffee. I've got better things to do, like type and file.

A. "Accidentally" spill some hot coffee in his lap once or twice. Blame your new behavior on "female troubles" —he'll be too embarrassed to ask for details.

•

Q. I've just discovered that my boss is having an affair with one of the executives in the accounting department. Should I take any action?

A. How about requesting some extra petty cash?

•

Q. My raise is way overdue, and I realize I have to take the initiative. What should I do? (My boss is one tough lady.)

A. Walk into your boss's office, shut the door, and quickly take off all of your clothes. Tell the bitch if she doesn't give you a raise, you'll scream rape.

•

Q. My boss keeps hounding me for a date and won't take no for an answer. How can I make him quit with the propositions without losing my job?

A. Tell him you're already sleeping with his boss.

•

Q. How can I get my secretary to stop chewing gum when she answers the phone? It sounds so tacky.

A. Hire someone with false teeth.

•

Q. My secretary is hopelessly ugly and I feel sorry for her. What would be an appropriate Christmas gift?

A. A variable-speed vibrator.

•

Q. On more than one occasion my boss has claimed client lunches at expensive restaurants on his expense account when in fact he was having a sandwich at his desk. I don't want to get fired, but I don't want to get hit for fraud either—should I confront him?

A.   Just pick a pricey restaurant and tell him you're a hungry new client.

•

Q.   My six-month review has come and gone, but my boss never said a word about it. Should I bring it up?

A.   Take the hint.

•

Q.   Many times when I answer the phone for my boss, I'll get someone on the line who is reluctant to give his name. Is this impolite on his part?

A.   Yes. Keep him on hold until he gives in.

•

Q.   When my boss shakes hands, it feels like I'm pumping a dishrag or a cube of Jell-O. How can I teach him how to shake hands properly?

A.   Tell him to wave "Hi" instead.

•

Q.   Our office is being computerized, and my secretary of thirty years is having trouble adapting. I feel bad, but I need to know when I should confront the problem and let her go.

A.   As soon as you see White-Out on her computer screen.

•

Q. My boss's breath is foul and I cringe every time he breathes in my direction. Should I mention this problem to him?

A. And lose your job? Pick up an inexpensive surgical mask instead.

•

Q. Should I accept a lunch invitation from my boss?

A. If you're prepared to be dessert.

•

Q. My boss says we have to cut back on expenses, so he wants me to share a hotel room with him during our next business trip. Is there a polite way of putting him off without jeopardizing my job?

A. No. Screw him and get it over with.

•

Q. On National Secretary's Day, my boss gave me a gift membership at the local fitness salon. Wasn't this impertinent?

A. Yes, but he has to look at you.

•

Q. I'm a little nervous about my new job since it's my first with a female boss. Any pointers for an ambitious guy?

A. Type fast and lick slowly.

•

Q. I'll be accompanying my boss on a business trip for the first time next month. What should I anticipate in the way of special arrangements?

A. Birth control.

•

Q. I'm a secretary, forty-five years old, not particularly attractive, a little overweight. I enjoy my job, but let's face it: the title "secretary" is pretty demeaning. People's eyes light up when I tell them the name of the company I work for, but cloud over again when they hear what my position is. Can this be avoided?

A. Don't tell them you're just a secretary. Tell them you're middle-aged, fat, and ugly, too.

Coworkers

Q. I see quite a few people roller-skating around the city. Would people think it odd if I roller-skated to my job?

A. Do you work for the circus?

•

Q. Should a man enter the elevator first and hold the Open button, or should he motion the woman to go ahead?

A. Why? You looking for a job?

•

Q. I love my job, but my boss's boss is starting to make it clear that if I don't give him some action on the side, my career will suffer. What can I do?

A. Wow, that really sucks! (So should you.)

•

Q. I'm the only woman executive in my company, and the men get a vicarious thrill out of embarrassing me during board meetings, belching and telling dirty jokes so they can watch me blush. What can I do?

A. *Truly Tasteless Jokes* Volumes I through VI are available in your local bookstore. Strike back.

•

Q. My coworkers leave the area around the coffee machine looking like a pig swill, and no one ever cleans up but me. Any suggestions?

A. Bitch, bitch, bitch.

•

Q. I can't stand company parties! The office is no place for sloppy and unprofessional behavior. How can I get the company to discontinue this disgusting custom?

A. Take pictures at the next one.

•

Q. Is it correct to proposition a potential client?

A. Yes, especially if you're a hooker.

•

Q. I'm in charge of dispensing bathroom keys to all the employees. Which key (His or Hers) should I give to a flaming faggot who swishes around the office with wrists so limp he can barely type?

A. Both.

•

Q. Isn't it rude of people to talk on the phone when you're in their office?

A. Yes, unless you have something to gain by eavesdropping.

•

Q. One of my coworkers has just moved to an office with a window and a bigger desk than mine. Should I be concerned?

A. Yes. His dick's probably bigger too, stubby.

•

Q. It always annoys me when secretaries ask primly, "May I ask what this is in reference to?" when I'm trying to get through to their bosses. Is this really necessary?

A. Yes. You can get right through to your party, though, with such answers as "It's about the great bondage scene we had last night," or "It's concerning the immediate repossession of his Coupe de Ville."

•

Q. Is it okay to make a reasonable number of personal phone calls from the office?

A. If you're the boss, yes.
If you're the grunt, no.
If you're the grunt and the boss is out of the office, yes.

•

Q.   Most of the clients I take out to lunch are men, and they feel uncomfortable when a woman picks up the tab. How should I pay without drawing too much attention?

A.   U.S. currency is accepted just about everywhere, as are most major credit cards.

•

Q.   I'm to address our sales conference for the first time, and any tips as to professional comportment would be appreciated.

A.   Loosen up your audience with a couple of truly tasteless jokes. (Volumes I through VI are available at your local bookstore.) Loosen yourself up with a couple shots of vodka.

•

Q.   What's a tactful way to get salespeople out of my office when they've overstayed their welcomes?

A.   Buy what they're selling.

•

Q.   When approaching a revolving door, should a man enter first and push, or let the woman pass in front of him?

A.   He should motion her to go ahead, then squeeze in the same compartment and feel her up while she can't move.

•

Q.   In my small company, people are constantly gossiping and backbiting. How can I put an end to this?

A.   Don't hire women.

•

Q. I happen to have a clock in my office, and several people regularly interrupt me to ask the time. What should I say?

A. How about, "The big hand is on the . . ."

•

Q. A woman in our office is a recent immigrant from Eastern Europe who wants to perfect her English and get rid of her accent. Should the rest of us correct her mistakes?

A. Yes, preferably in front of her superiors.

•

Q. My boss chastised me for complimenting a fellow attorney on his new suit. He said it was unprofessional, but I don't see anything wrong with an occasional word of praise, do you?

A. Compliment his briefs, not what's in them.

Leaving the Job

Q. How should I answer a potential employer if he asks me why I left my job when in fact I was fired?

A. Lie.

•

Q. What is the proper way to confront a boss who refuses to write a letter of recommendation because he's upset I'm leaving?

A. Forget confronting—forge it.

•

Q. Isn't it impolite to use those desk speakerphones for personal conversations? Whenever I call, I feel as though our private conversation is being broadcast over the whole office.

A. So don't talk dirty.

•

Q. What is the best way to close a business letter to a prospective client?

A. Lick the gummy flap and fold it shut.

•

Q. Is it appropriate to send Christmas cards to fellow office workers?

A. Only if you have no other friends.

•

Q. Isn't it rude to cover the mouth of the phone to talk to someone else?

A. No. How else are you going to get your stories straight?

•

Q. There's this guy who wears pants so tight you can see everything, and I mean everything. Isn't this in poor taste at the office?

A. So get together *after* work.

•

Q. In good weather I bicycle to work. Is it indecorous to wear a skirt?

A. No. Just wear clean underwear in case of an accident.

•

Q. I have great legs and would like to show them off in short shorts at our annual company picnic. Would this be inappropriate?

A. No. Sit across from your boss.

•

Q. Is it appropriate to wear rubbers to the office on those really rainy days?

A. Sure. By the way, doesn't your dick work on sunny days?

Dress

Did Tarzan have to worry about what to wear as long as his schlong wasn't hanging out? Did Cheetah have to worry about anything besides becoming a fur coat? (Luckily, Jane wasn't Jewish.)

But things have "evolved" since then: now we all have closets full of clothes, none of which is ever appropriate for the next event on our social calendar. Let Blanche show you how to get by with last year's monkey suit, or when it's proper to wear those stained crotchless undies, and you'll feel comfortable at any occasion.

———

Q. Although I live in the East, my everyday work clothes consist of a suit, boots, and a cowboy hat. May I wear my hat indoors?

A. Hemorrhoids and cowboy hats have a lot in common: sooner or later every asshole has one.

•

Q. When should one wear white gloves?

A. When shaking hands with black people. Also, in no case should they be removed *before* a dinner guest has attended to her host's sexual needs.

•

Q. I'm a Polish citizen and I don't understand the difference between "formal," "semi-formal," and "casual" dress. Can you help me?

A. In this order: A clean, ironed bowling shirt; a clean bowling shirt; and a bowling shirt that's been worn for at least three days straight.

•

Q. I've been given a beautiful and quite expensive pink ruffled tuxedo shirt. For what social occasion should I wear it?

A. An AIDS fund-raising party in Italy.

•

Q. Should black people wear black tie to a formal affair?

A. No. You can't tell where the skin begins and it makes the lower lip look even bigger.

•

Q. After a rape, is it my responsibility to replace the clothes that I tore or soiled?

A. No. A gentleman never buys clothes for a woman to whom he has not been properly introduced!

•

Q.   I was quite shocked to see people sunbathing in my local park wearing next to nothing. Isn't the beach the place for bikinis?

A.   Yes. Don't go there either, you prude.

•

Q.   When may a man wear an ascot or knotted scarf instead of a necktie?

A.   Anytime he feels like displaying his homosexual tendencies.

•

Q.   What do you think about three-year-old girls in bikinis? Aren't they just too young to be so scantily clad?

A.   Oooh! Don't tease me!

•

Q.   If a woman is taller than her date, should she wear flats?

A.   It's better than being seen with a nerd wearing elevator shoes.

•

Q.   When, if ever, should a woman wear a hat?

A.   When she's undergoing chemotherapy.

•

Q.   I know I'm old-fashioned, but it doesn't seem proper for my daughter to go about braless. She says nobody even notices. Who's right?

A. If no one's noticing, treat her to a silicone implant.

•

Q. I have my eye on a beautiful—but quite revealing—evening dress. How much cleavage is too much?

A. Depends on the size of your jugs.

•

Q. Is it acceptable to wear a dark suit to a black-tie occasion?

A. Sure, cheapskate.

•

Q. What's the difference between black tie and white tie?

A. What are you, blind?

•

Q. I've been invited to a formal reception starting at 5 P.M. Must I wear a long dress?

A. Only if you've stopped shaving your legs.

•

Q. My husband wants to give me a mink wrap for our anniversary, but I find furs pretentious at all but the most formal occasions. What do you think?

A. Don't be a fool. A fur isn't a fashion statement, it's a financial one.

•

Q.   Where should a man put his hat when at the movies?

A.   If the film's X-rated, on his lap, over the hankie.

•

Q.   Is it *de rigueur* to wear brown shoes with a navy blue suit?

A.   If you mean *fucked up,* yes.

•

Q.   Is it all right for a man to wear a single earring with a conservative three-piece suit and short hair?

A.   Depends on the height of his pumps.

•

Q.   When does one wear a white tie and tails?

A.   When playing the piano or imitating a penguin.

•

Q.   Is it all right to be wearing a nightgown when Room Service arrives?

A.   Yes, if the meal is breakfast or the waiter's exceptionally cute.

•

Q.   Do I really have to wear those unfeminine business suits in order to "dress for success"?

A.   Yes, because you're fat and ugly. No one good-looking would ask that question.

•

Q. Isn't it unprofessional-looking for women to change into tennis shoes at 5:00? My feet may hurt, but I don't take off my heels till I'm home.

A. If you're Puerto Rican, those strappy leetle numbers with fuck-me heels *are* running shoes.

•

Q. I know dressing correctly for the job is very important. What can I wear that would be feminine but not provocative?

A. A padded bra.

•

Q. Some of our Sicilian neighbors always wear hats, indoors and out, no matter what the occasion. Is there some point of etiquette which accounts for this, or is it purely an ethnic question?

A. Neither—they wear hats so they'll know which end to wipe.

•

Q. The bosomy salesgirl in the lingerie store kept staring at my front, and practically sniggered when I requested something in an A cup. Wasn't she being awfully rude?

A. Yes, but can you blame her?

•

Q. Should a man point out to a woman that her bra strap is showing, and if so, how?

A. Snap it.

Fitness

My idea of exercise is hefting a few dry vodka martinis and fishing out the olives when I'm done. After all, only cheap sluts wear skintight clothes, and who says cellulite isn't a turn-on?

Why you narcissists and masochists want to spend a lot of time and money torturing yourselves is beyond me. Ditch the barbells and bring back the singles bars. And ladies, stop worrying about reps and shinsplints and whether sweat is streaking your makeup, because it is, and you look ridiculous.

Q. I belong to an exclusive, all-male health club and find it strange that members are required to swim naked in the swimming pool. Why is this?

A. How else are they going to tell if any Jews sneak in?

•

Q. A couple of blacks have started jogging in our neighborhood. How can I persuade them to run elsewhere?

A. Shout, "Stop, thief!"

•

Q.   Is it socially acceptable for a man to use the Jane Fonda workout cassette?

A.   It's like riding a moped or fucking a fat girl: fine until someone sees you.

•

Q.   Is badminton considered a manly sport?

A.   Since it features a "birdie" or a "shuttlecock," what do you think?

•

Q.   A gay friend is thinking of joining my health club and wants to check out the facilities. What games should we play?

A.   Hide the weenie, if you're adventurous.

•

Q.   I understand Jews are not very athletic. Isn't there some sport I can talk to my Jewish friends about?

A.   Yes; matzoh ball.

•

Q.   Is it socially acceptable to burp and fart while working out in the gym?

A.   Sure, and why don't you pick your nose and eat it while you're at it?

•

Q. What is the correct jogging garb in the city?

A. Shorts and a T-shirt, unless you're Puerto Rican. If so, wear polyester and carry a television.

•

Q. My boss has asked me to be his guest at his racquetball club. He is a very competitive person, and I'm not sure how he'll react if I beat him. What should I do?

A. It sounds obvious enough to me.

•

Q. I just found out my health club doesn't admit blacks. Should I say something to the admissions committee?

A. No. Blacks don't need health clubs; they get plenty of exercise from manual labor.

•

Q. After a workout, should I shower before or after my Perrier and lime at the health bar?

A. What a wonderfully stupid question.

•

Q. Is it okay to ask if you can borrow someone's shampoo in the club showers?

A. Yes, as long as the person doesn't ask you to pick his bar of soap up off the floor in return.

•

Q. A business associate just invited me to go to "the baths" with him. Is this some kind of health club? And should I accept?

A. Why not? To be on the safe side, use soap on a rope.

•

Q. Sometime when I work out, the dumbbells make me strain and I inadvertently pass gas. Should I excuse myself?

A. No. Follow it up with a manly sigh of relief.

•

Q. When running on a track, who should yield right-of-way, a jogger or someone in a wheelchair?

A. The wheelchair. Rolling is not running.

•

Q. A friend of mine recently lost a leg, but he refuses to give up jogging and is constantly asking me to "run" with him. Do I have to slow down to accommodate his new pace?

A. No. Tell him you're out for a run, not a hop. Buy him a pet frog if he still insists.

•

Q. I belong to a very exclusive health club that two friends want to join. They both have the same qualifications, but one is Jewish. What should I say to the Jew when he finds out he didn't make it?

A. "Oi vey!"

•

Q.   Should I spot for a woman even if she doesn't ask for assistance?

A.   How else are you going to see her tits at close range?

•

Q.   A friend works out practically every day but only washes his gym clothes about once a month. Should I say something?

A.   Yes, over the phone.

•

Q.   My aerobics class is full of fat, dumpy women, and I'm disgusted being in the same room with them. Should I sprinkle around some comments about obesity or just grin and bear it?

A.   Sprinkle away, and I hope you get sat on—God! I hate skinny women!

•

Q.   At least fifty percent of all social conversation centers on weight versus height, number of push-ups, amounts of weight lifted while bench-pressing, etc. These people are just as obnoxious as born-again Christians. Why can't they be more courteous and stop preaching?

A.   Calm down and have another Twinkie, dearie.

•

Q.   I usually wear a bodysuit when I work out, and find men are constantly leering at me. What should I do to discourage their behavior?

A.   Cover your tits with a sweatshirt and your lips with a pair of shorts.

•

Q.   I've just joined a coed health club and am embarrassed that I get a huge erection around all those scantily clad women. What should I do?

A.   Lift weights with it.

•

Q.   If a woman is having difficulties lifting the dumbbells, is it polite to volunteer to help, or am I being sexist?

A.   You're being sexist—she's probably a dyke, anyway.

•

Q.   These coed gyms confuse me. Should a guy give up his Nautilus to a chick waiting in line?

A.   No, though you can offer to wrestle her for it.

•

Q.   My mom gave me a membership at the local health club for my birthday (I've been putting on a few pounds lately), and I'm real nervous about my first visit. What should I wear?

A.   Something baggy.

•

Q.   I come to my health club to work out, but all these other women are just here to meet guys. The sauna smells like a whorehouse, and most of them wouldn't know the difference between Ben Gay and Ban Roll-On. What can I do?

A.   Use the men's room. (It's a great way to meet guys, too.)

•

Q.   I think my girl friend is overweight. Is there a polite way to tell her without her getting upset?

A.   First see if you can still hear the stereo when she's sitting on your face.

•

Q.   What is proper etiquette for jogging on a crowded city street?

A.   Avoid pedestrians, unless it slows you down.

•

Q.   A good friend and devoted jogger just had both legs amputated after a snowmobile accident. What can I give him?

A.   A pair of expensive running shoes in your size.

•

Q.   My girlfriend is constantly asking me to jog with her, but she's just too slow. Would it be rude to ask her to find someone else to jog with?

A.   No, but don't be surprised if she finds someone else to sleep with, too.

•

Q.   A close friend recently had a facelift and obviously expects compliments on her youthful appearance. I think she looks like a death's-head. What should I say to her?

A.   "I'm so sorry."

•

Q.   A wealthy friend frequently invites me to spend the day sailing with him. I can't afford a boat but would like to reciprocate in some way—what would be appropriate?

A.   Give him a blow job.

•

Q.   Is it rude to boo your home team when it's playing really poorly?

A.   Yes. It's more satisfying to throw things.

•

Q.   When attending a sporting event, who should be responsible for obtaining refreshments for the group?

A.   The butler.

•

Q.   Is there a polite way to tell a friend she's too fat?

A.   Try "Hey fatso, take human bites!"

•

Q.   Is it indiscreet to ask someone who their dermatologist is?

A.   Of course, zitface.

•

Q.   My boyfriend gave me a one-year subscription to a local health club, but I'd sooner die than work out. Should I return his gift?

A.   Take the hint, fatty.

•

Q.   My jogging partner is much slower than I. How can I politely let him know that I think it's time I started running alone?

A.   Take him for a run in Harlem in the dead of night.

•

Q.   Should one tip all the attendants in a beauty parlor?

A.   Depends on how extensive the repairs were, toadface.

Dating

I wanted to call this chapter "Free Fucking," but my publisher wouldn't let me. Still, I'm not being prescient when I say the etiquette of dating has changed radically. Sexually transmitted diseases have put a new twist on things, except for those who like risks and rubbers; it's one thing to tell your date you have herpes, and quite another to let your wife know you have AIDS. Used to be that guys went out with gals, but you can't even count on that now. In fact, the only difference between dating and prostitution is that prostitution's more lucrative.

But, hey, if your idea of a wild time lately's been a pint of Haagen Dazs on a Saturday night, what've you got to lose?

———————

Q. If a guy gives his fraternity pin to a girl, does that mean they're engaged?

A. If you mean, "Are they fucking?" the answer's yes.

•

Q. My teenage friends like to drink and drive. I don't drink and I'm scared to death we'll have an accident, but I don't want my friends to think I'm a chicken. Is there a polite way to get out of going on these little "joyrides"?

A. Not at your age.

•

Q. I have a crush on a boy in my class. Would it be too forward of me to call and ask him for a date?

A. No. Just be prepared to put out.

•

Q. Is it all right to give my boyfriend a snapshot of me to take with him into the army? If so, should I sign it?

A. Yes. Head shots are nice, but a crotch shot will keep his interest longer. Sign it: "This can be yours if you come home without the clap."

•

Q. What's the best way to let someone know his fly is open?

A. Point and giggle.

•

Q. Friends snicker when I tell them I met my boyfriend through a notice in our local paper. What's so funny?

A. You had to *advertise* for a date!?!

•

Q.   I'm lonely and eager to meet someone, but as I'm also rather inexperienced, I'm not sure what would be the correct way to go about it. Can you help?

A.   Put an ad in the paper under "Positions Wanted."

•

Q.   I've been asked to meet my girlfriend's family. What should I wear?

A.   A flak jacket.

•

Q.   A good friend is dating a guy I can't stand. Would it be wrong to tell her how I feel?

A.   Go ahead. Find out how good a friend she really is.

•

Q.   What is the correct way to put off an overly zealous suitor's amorous advances? I'm not particularly interested in a romantic relationship.

A.   Ask if it's in yet.

•

Q.   My mom doesn't approve of my fiancé, so she never gets his name straight—it's Joe, John, or Jerry (his name is Joel). What can I do?

A.   Call her "Bitch" until her memory improves.

•

Q.   My fiancé's family lives on the wrong side of the tracks, literally and figuratively. I know they're too shy to meet my family because each of my invitations has been met with a flat refusal. Should I continue to pursue this get-together at all costs?

A. Hire them to work around your parents' place: Mom can cook and clean, Dad can chauffeur, and the kids can look after the yard.

•

Q. I was crushed when none of the girls noticed my new engagement ring at work on Monday. What can I say that's subtle but will do the trick?

A. How about, "Gee it's hot in here—I think I'll take my ring off."

•

Q. How can I politely ask my roommate to leave us alone when I'm in the company of a potential boyfriend and she decides to join us?

A. Hiss, "Am-scray, itch-bay."

•

Q. I want to give my girlfriend an engagement ring. Is there a right time or place?

A. Before she's pregnant, and on her finger.

•

Q. Is there a polite way to give a guy the brush-off?

A. No. Should there be?

•

Q. How can I get out of my roommate's well-meaning attempts to set me up with a blind date?

A. Give it a chance: if she's ugly, she's probably horny. If she's *really* ugly, slip her into a body bag before you start humping.

•

Q. I'm sixteen years of age, and every time I ask a girl out she comes up with an excuse or just says, "No, you ugly toad." Okay, I'm not the handsomest guy in the world, but I think these girls are being pretty rude. What tack should I take next?

A. Try the next dance at Lighthouse for the Blind.

•

Q. Are there any occasions these days when kissing a woman's hand is appropriate?

A. No. She'll think you missed her lips.

•

Q. Under what circumstances should a man take a woman's elbow to guide her across the street?

A. If she is blind or older than his mother.

•

Q. When should you give a girl flowers?

A. When your father's a florist.

•

Q. Is door-to-door service required these days—picking your date up at home and seeing her safely back to her place?

A. Don't you want to get laid?

•

Q. Would you tell a woman in advance where you're taking her on a date?

A. I don't date women.

•

Q. When is it appropriate to take a date bowling?

A. When she's wearing a miniskirt.

•

Q. Is it considered good manners to ask your date if you can kiss her on a first date?

A. If you have to ask, you're in deep trouble. Better, wait for a quiet, romantic moment and say: "Would you like to lick my dick?" Or: "Does the number sixty-nine have any special meaning for you?"

•

Q. My boyfriend is almost two feet taller than I am, and people are constantly making the same dumb quips about our sex life, etc. Isn't this rude?

A. Very. Incidentally, can you kiss and screw at the same time?

•

Q. In these liberated times, can a woman ask a man to dance?

A. How else would fat girls get out on the dance floor?

•

Q. I'm dating this woman who's already been given plenty of perfume and chocolate. Is it okay to give her clothes instead?

A. Dummy, you're supposed to try to get *into* her pants. Why make it harder on yourself?

•

Q. When does a gentleman offer his arm to a lady?

A. When she's missing one.

•

Q. My girlfriend's family says a lengthy grace before each meal. I was not brought up in a religious household and am not sure how to behave.

A. Feel your girlfriend up under the table while she can't squirm.

•

Q. What's the proper way to thank a prostitute for an evening's entertainment?

A. Try cash.

•

Q. After purchasing the services of a "lady of the evening," should I take her out for refreshments?

A. Yes, unless you got a blow job, in which case it's not necessary.

•

Q. How should a prostitute be properly addressed?

A. "Yo, mama."

•

Q. When eliciting the services of a prostitute, should one pay before or after?

A. Pay before and the trick's on you, buddy.

•

Q. Should I stay to the outside of the sidewalk when strolling with a woman?

A. Who the hell strolls anymore?

•

Q. Recently, while a woman friend was busy in the kitchen making dinner, the phone rang. I answered and was greeted by a male voice asking for her. How should I have responded?

A. "Sorry, wrong number."

•

Q. Is it my responsibility to tell my date what to wear to a dinner party given by friends of mine she doesn't know?

A. No. Judge her by her selection.

•

Q.   Is there a polite way to tell a guy "no"? I want to save myself until I get married.

A.   With that attitude, you'll be "saving yourself" for yourself.

•

Q.   I'm embarrassed to even bring this up, but I can't think of anyone else to ask. Why is it called a *blow job?*

A.   Because it's so embarrassing if you blow it.

•

Q.   How far ahead is it okay to ask a girl out for a date?

A.   If she's fat or ugly, try five to ten minutes.

•

Q.   I've invited this girl I like out to dinner twice, but she's been busy. Still, she sounds pleased that I called. How many more times is it polite to try?

A.   Since subtlety isn't one of your talents, keep trying until she says something like: "Sorry, not tonight, my hair hurts."

•

Q.   I know it's become socially acceptable to become lovers after the first or second date, but I'm an old-fashioned guy who prefers to know a woman first. Isn't this perfectly appropriate?

A. How are you going to get to know her if you don't fuck her, idiot?

•

Q. How do you know if a girl wants you to kiss her after a first date or not? I don't want to be rude.

A. She'll let you know. Wear a metal jockstrap just in case.

•

Q. How long must one wait before asking a woman for a date after she has broken up with a friend?

A. Who said anything about waiting?

•

Q. If you've drunk too much on a date and feel as if you're going to be sick, what's the correct way to handle the problem?

A. If you're a woman, steer clear of blow jobs. If you're a male, ask for a blow job, and while she's sucking away discreetly barf in a nearby ashtray.

•

Q. Is it impolite to ask to drive on a date, even though I'm a girl?

A. If you drive, who's going to give him head?

•

Q. My prom date is picking me up on his motorcycle. Should I wear my long dress, or would you recommend changing once we get to the dance?

A. Wear your prom dress, and a jockstrap underneath so you don't whistle at high speeds.

●

Q. My girl friend wears bras which are impossible to open without "ruining the mood." Can you suggest a proper way of undoing the straps while maintaining the atmosphere?

A. Weren't you ever a Boy Scout? Be prepared—carry a knife.

(P.S. A knife is a great tool to help get a prudish woman "in the mood.")

●

Q. During sex, my boyfriend asks me to go down on him. I comply, but I end up gagging and he loses his erection. Is there a correct way to give a blow job?

A. Just close your eyes and pretend you're sucking a lollipop that squirts.

●

Q. My boyfriend tells me I'm not giving a proper blow job because he winces every time I start to suck him. Is there such a thing as sucking etiquette?

A. Try not using your teeth.

●

Q. I'm fourteen years old and still a virgin. My boyfriend tells me not to worry because he has a condom. Would it be rude to ask to see it? And why should where he lives make a difference? Is a condom safer than a house or a summer cottage?

A.   Are you sure you're still a virgin?

•

Q.   When I call a girl's house to ask her out and one of her parents answers the phone, should I introduce myself?

A.   No, make them guess.

•

Q.   We're only fifteen, so my boyfriend and I have to be driven around by one of our parents. Who should sit where in the car?

A.   Make the chaperone business as unpleasant as possible. Sit in the backseat and feel each other up. Tell your parents to keep their eyes on the road.

•

Q.   I've just started French kissing and need to know where the spit should go. I don't want to dribble on my boyfriend.

A.   Swallow. This will make you even more popular later on.

•

Q.   I've decided to come out of the closet and cruise the gay bars. What is proper cruising etiquette for picking up a fellow homosexual?

A.   So you want some cruising aid, huh? Start with a note from your doctor pasted on your ass if you're a slave type; your dick, if you're into being the master.

•

Q.   Is it okay to eat out on the first date?

A.   Give it your best shot. I'd try for an old-fashioned French kiss if I were you.

Travel

Whoever said, "Getting there is half the fun," must have been a car salesman. When was the last time you enjoyed sitting in a traffic jam on your way to some jive-ass job?

Transportation, especially during rush hours, has one all-encompassing rule: survival of the fittest. Call it etiquette if you wish. People who insist on some sort of protocol are usually the ones crowded out of the subway car. And they deserve it.

———————

Q. People often take up seats on the train with their clothing and luggage. It is impolite to ask them to make room so I can sit down?

A. No, but don't take it personally if they tell you to piss off.

•

Q. Shouldn't people boarding a subway train let people out before crowding into the car themselves?

A.   No known rules of civilized behavior apply to underground transportation.

•

Q.   My boyfriend is very aggressive behind the wheel and often flips the bird out the window at other drivers who annoy him. Isn't this rather extreme?

A.   Yes, but if your boyfriend is black and an ex-con, you have nothing to worry about.

•

Q.   Since he lives at home, my little brother is always using the backseat of my car for his romantic rendezvous, and it's starting to smell like a fish market. Shouldn't he clean up after himself, and maybe buy me some gas occasionally?

A.   Be grateful he's not staining your sheets.

•

Q.   Every now and then I run into people on the subway that I don't want to talk to. Would it be impolite to bury my nose in a book to avoid any conversational assaults?

A.   No, but don't be surprised when a group of blacks do some assaulting of their own.

•

Q.   Buses and subway cars are continually strewn with litter: newspapers, candy wrappers, tissues, and so on. I think it's terrible that people don't pick up after themselves or, worse, purposely discard their reading material and trash. How can they be so discourteous?

A.   You get what you pay for. Take a cab.

•

Q.   Should a man give up his seat for a pregnant woman?

A.   No, but a woman should—she might get knocked up herself someday.

•

Q.   Crowded buses or subway cars are breeding grounds for the occasional lascivious pinch or poke. How can I best deflect this juvenile behavior?

A.   Yell, "Get your filthy hands off me or I'll cut off your balls."

•

Q.   Some subway riders smell as though they haven't bathed in weeks, and the rest of us are too grossed out to stand anywhere near them. Shouldn't these people be more considerate?

A.   Why? It's a great way to get a seat in rush hour.

•

Q.   If I by chance meet a lady friend taking the same train, should I offer to pay for her ticket?

A.   No way. But if you knock her up, you should chip in for the abortion.

•

Q. I'm nervous about traveling on the subway and would like to protect myself. What would be the correct firearm?

A. A Saturday night special: easy to find, good at point-blank range, and ammunition is readily available. Just ask Bernie Goetz.

•

Q. When leaving my hotel, I'm usually accosted by a burly doorman who seems to expect a tip for summoning a taxi. Should I give him something even when the cabs are lined up down the block and all he has to do is wave his arm?

A. No. But be careful in New York City, where doormen beat up people like you.

•

Q. Under what circumstances is it okay to give a taxi driver directions?

A. If he's too drunk to drive.

•

Q. I hate it when cars block the crosswalk. Is there a proper response to this rudeness?

A. A rock through the windshield is usually appropriate.

•

Q. I'm confused. When entering a bus or train, do I go in before or after a woman struggling with her luggage; and when leaving, does she exit before or after me?

A.   Unless you're practicing to be a porter, forget about it.

•

Q.   Should the stewardess ever be tipped?

A.   No. Proposition her outright.

•

Q.   On planes I always seem to get seated next to blabbermouths. Is it rude simply to tell them I'm not in the mood for conversation?

A.   No. Or ask if you can borrow their airsickness bag.

•

Q.   Isn't it good manners to clean up after yourself in an airplane bathroom?

A.   If you want "chambermaid" on your resumé.

•

Q.   Should I give up my seat to accommodate a mother traveling with her child?

A.   No. Let the brat ruin someone else's trip.

•

Q.   Is there a polite way to get a backseat driver to shut up?

A.   Insist on looking at the person while he's talking.

●

Q.   How do you feel about people who swipe office stationery and hotel towels?

A.   Just fine, unless it's my house they're visiting.

●

Q.   Should a couple traveling together register as "Mr. & Mrs." to avoid embarrassment?

A.   Sure, unless they're both males.

●

Q.   On my upcoming business trip to Japan, will I be required to bow to my new associates?

A.   Certainly. How else are you going to see them?

●

Q.   If I'm taking my girlfriend to a motel for the night, how should I sign the register?

A.   "Mr. and Mrs. John Doe." Unless, of course, that's your real name.

●

Q.   Is it appropriate for a woman traveling alone on business to have drinks in the hotel bar or dinner in the restaurant?

A.   Sure, especially if she's horny.

●

Q.   When a taxi has been hailed, is it more polite for me to hold the curbside door for my date, thus obliging her to scoot awkwardly across the seat, or to get in first myself?

A.   Make her get in first unless it's raining.

PART IV

Especially
Delicate
Social Matters

So you like the taste of your own boogers? How about the smell of your own farts? Ahh, this is what I call etiquette. Still, if you want to know how to broach these sensitive subjects and others like them, this chapter's for you, especially the *Nasty Habits* section.

Find out once and for all how polite you really have to be to people in the hospital (somewhat—they may recover), to old people (not very), and to people in wheelchairs (not at all—what're they going to do about it? Chase you?).

"But Blanche," you say, "there're scores of etiquette books in the bookstores already. What can you offer that those others don't?" Good question.

Babies

A lot of people jump into this baby business just to prove they're not homos or that they really do screw their wives occasionally. It's not worth it.

First of all, babies are hideous to anyone but their parents and horribly noisy unless they are stillborn, in which case they begin to smell after a week or two. Babies are also utterly helpless and extremely expensive, and this makes sensible adults hostile and resentful. The best way to avoid these negative feelings is contraception. If it's too late for that, give your child up for adoption (you can make a bundle if it's white) or "forget" to babyproof the house. If you're too squeamish for that, then keep the child sedated and preferably out of sight until it's old enough for full-time day care at, say, three months. Make its first word not "Dada" but "scholarship." And read this chapter carefully so you are sure to stay within the boundaries of etiquette—or do I mean the law?

Q. When should a parent start carrying around baby pictures? My wife had to have a sonogram done when the fetus was only about the size of a coffee bean, and my mother-in-law is insisting on a wallet-size print.

A. Give her one. At this point the baby resembles an unripe lizard, so you can point out the family resemblance.

•

Q. Friends of ours are about to adopt a black baby. What present should I get for the child?

A. A pacifier that won't squish its nose down any further.

•

Q. When is it appropriate to announce one's pregnancy?

A. Just before it begins to announce itself.

•

Q. I have noticed that Oriental babies are far better behaved than Western ones. Is there a proper way to educate my child in the same fashion?

A. Orientals live in very small apartments where someone is always holding the child because there is no place to put it down.

•

Q. It has been my experience that pregnant women and new parents lose all sense of humor about their situation and their new offspring. Am I acting incorrectly when I try to lighten things up a bit?

A. Absolutely not. Dead baby jokes are appropriate up until the child is several months old—while the risk of crib death is still high.

•

Q.   I plan to breast-feed my baby. Is it okay nowadays to do it in public?

A.   Do you live in Africa? Anyone not recently featured in *National Geographic* should be reluctant to publicly display their similarity to a dairy cow.

•

Q.   An acquaintance of mine gave birth to a mongoloid idiot. Is there an appropriate gift or card for this sad occasion?

A.   1. Tickets to the next Special Olympics.
      2. A condolence card.
      3. A coat hanger so that it doesn't happen again.

•

Q.   My niece brings her little terror along whenever she comes to visit. I shut him in the bathroom "by accident" once, and he filled the toilet with all my sanitary napkins and it still doesn't flush right. Is it up to me to house-train her kid?

A.   Not if you pull the bathroom trick again and don't use those pesky childproof bottles.

•

Q.   Is it really necessary to whisk the baby into another room when changing it? It's only a little baby.

A.   Shit is shit, and nothing is cute when covered in it.

•

Q. We hear that friends just produced a baby so ugly it makes Howard Cosell look like Adonis. What's a tactful comment on first viewing?

A. The approved response is, "My, that *is* a baby!" However, it is best to discourage the couple from further procreation. Try "What drugs did you take during pregnancy?"; "Who dropped it?"; or a simple, "I'm so sorry."

•

Q. Whatever happened to all those thalidomide babies?

A. Automobile manufacturers use them to test airbags.

•

Q. My husband and I just adopted a Korean baby girl. What should we do when people comment that she doesn't look like us?

A. Act surprised.

•

Q. We were shocked to come home and find our three-year-old daughter lying spread-legged on the living room floor being enthusiastically licked by our neighbor's German shepherd. How should we handle this with our neighbors?

A. Unless your daughter is big for her age, suggest they get a smaller dog before things get serious.

•

Q. Is it a no-no to order stuff for the baby before the birth? Some people seem superstitious about it.

A.   You can write it off if the baby's stillborn. Check with your accountant.

•

Q.   Our best friends are both dark-haired and brown-eyed, and she's just given birth to the fairest, blondest baby I've ever seen. What should we say to them?

A.   "What a beautiful baby—whose is it?"

•

Q.   Mothers are always handing me their drooling, puking little brats to hold. How can I gracefully escape these duties?

A.   Drop one or two.

•

Q.   Our two-year-old daughter is very late in the hair department, so even if she's dressed in frills and lace, strangers come up and call her "Baldy" or "Bub" and it hurts her feelings. How can I put a stop to it?

A.   Tell people the hair loss is due to chemotherapy.

•

Q.   My brother-in-law was shocked when I gave his three-year-old daughter an "anatomically correct" doll for Christmas. Did I act incorrectly?

A.   Not at all. Now she can point out where it hurts when she's sexually abused in nursery school.

•

Q.   Friends of ours take their baby with them everywhere, and I mean everywhere. It's getting tiresome—is
there some way to break them of this habit?

A.   Take them scuba-diving.

•

Q.   A friend dropped by with her new baby and was
outraged when I lit up a cigarette. Was I being thoughtless?

A.   In your own house you can do anything you please,
short of setting the baby on fire. Save that till the second
visit.

•

Q.   My husband and I enjoy our life-style and have no
desire to have children, but people never seem to believe
this. Is there any way to cut down on their rude questions
as to when or why?

A.   No, so make it easy on yourself. Send Sally Struthers
a couple of bucks and buy a picture of some Third World
kid for your wallet.

•

Q.   Is "natural birth" the same for all religions?

A.   No. A JAP's version of "natural birth" means *absolutely* no makeup.

•

Q.   When friends come over for dinner, should I keep my
baby in the playpen or let it crawl around?

A.   Put the baby in the playpen and the playpen in the swimming pool.

•

Q.   When is it okay to spank a child in public?

A.   Whenever you're in the mood.

•

Q.   During warm weather my husband and I walk around the house naked. Can we continue to do so once our baby's born?

A.   After the first few months you should wear diapers so the baby doesn't feel "different."

•

Q.   My doctor says that since I'm going to have a baby I should get rid of our superbly trained Doberman—since the dog is capable of feeling jealousy and may attack the child. What should I do?

A.   Consider an abortion. Getting knocked up is easy, but training a good attack dog takes years.

•

Q.   Our friends have a four-year-old who still sleeps in the same bed with them. Is this healthy?

A.   As long as the child is still a virgin.

•

Q.   My stepson married a lovely black woman and they've just had their first child. Should I give it a black doll or a white one?

A.   Give it one of each and see if the kid makes the black one wait on the white one.

•

Q.   My daughter and son-in-law cannot have children and I'm continually being asked by people if I'm "going to be a grandmother soon" or "are there any babies expected?" I can't tell you how depressed those questions make me. Is it okay to tell these people to mind their own business?

A.   Yes. Ask them when they last got laid or if the story about their son's homosexuality is true.

•

Q.   This is our three-month-old's first Christmas. We were wondering if we should buy a tree. We haven't in the past.

A.   Fine, unless you're Jewish.

•

Q.   My husband's brother is a bit clumsy, and every time he picks up our baby my heart leaps into my throat. Should I communicate my fears to him?

A.   Yes, but make him put the kid down first.

•

Q.   What should I say to an expectant mother who doesn't really want the child? She keeps saying, "I didn't plan on this" or "I can't deal with more diapers."

A.   Remind her that she can exchange her "bundle of joy" for a bundle of cash on the black market. Offer to handle it for a small broker's fee.

•

Q.   A good friend was set on having a baby boy, and now that it's a girl he's very depressed. How can I show my support?

A.   Tell him he should be glad it's not deformed.

•

Q.   A good friend was set on having a baby girl, and now that it's a boy she's very depressed. How can I show my support?

A.   Tell her the kid looks gay and present it with a little silver vibrator and a jar of Vaseline.

•

Q.   Our parents can't accept the fact that our child is going to call us by our first names instead of "Mummy" and "Papa." Should my husband and I insist?

A.   Anything's better than calling yourself "Mummy" and "Papa," unless it's Adolf and Eva.

•

Q.   Many of my friends have babies and are beginning to compare one to the other—"Is yours walking yet?"; "Can yours sit up by itself?"; "Is yours eating solids?"; etc. It's becoming very competitive and ugly. Should I say anything?

A.   No. And I'm sorry your child is retarded.

•

Q. Child abuse is a big problem now and I'm afraid to leave my baby daughter with a male, but our next-door neighbor's son needs the money. How should I handle it?

A. Unless the kid gets a hard-on when he walks in the door, don't worry about it.

•

Q. Friends of ours breast-feed their child at the dinner table when they are entertaining guests. The breast-feeding doesn't bother me, but I find that the burping afterwards makes me queasy. Should I say anything?

A. You can if you feel like it—but why are you burping?

•

Q. Friends just had their first child. The baby wasn't planned, but I'd like to congratulate them anyway. What should I give them?

A. A box of Trojans.

•

Q. My mother-in-law is constantly telling me how to take care of my baby. Sometimes her advice is good, but most of the time it's just plain dumb. How can I politely tell her to butt out?

A. Point out her son's inadequacies.

•

Q. My brother and his wife are about to have their second child. Of course, their three-year-old son is curious and keeps asking how and when his brother or sister will arrive. Instead of telling the child the truth, they told him Mr. Stork will deliver the newborn about the time my sister-in-law is due. I think that this lie is going to damage the boy's psyche. Would it be proper to say something to either the parents or to my nephew?

A.   Mr. Stork is a lie?!?

•

Q.   Both of our parents are nuts about our newborn, but we're afraid the child will be spoiled. How can we remedy this problem?

A.   Put the baby in the freezer. That usually keeps them fresh.

•

Q.   Friends have just lost their first baby during a very difficult delivery. What would be an appropriate condolence gift?

A.   A dead puppy.

•

Q.   Some good friends chipped in and bought me a set of expensive stuffed animals, but I would prefer to return them for something useful like food. Would it be insensitive to ask them for the receipt?

A.   How else are you going to know what they spent?

•

Q.   I can't understand why my wife's so obsessed with her pregnancy—the topic's driving me crazy. Shouldn't she control her baby talk, and not bore people at social gatherings?

A.   ZZZZZZZZZZZZZZZZZ

•

Q.   Should we allow our child to call our friends by their first names, or insist on Mr.—— or Mrs.——?

A.   Surnames are fine if you're raising your child to be a menial.

•

Q.   My husband doesn't want me to use any painkillers while I'm in labor, but I understand the birthing process can be very painful and I'm scared. Is there a way to suggest that I may need some medication?

A.   Wait till he gets a case of hemorrhoids and hide the Preparation H.

•

Q.   Whenever today's "feeling" man gets on the topic of childbirth, he describes it as a shared experience—when, in fact, the woman was the one going through the pain. How can he be made aware of what the process really feels like?

A.   See if he can pull his lips over his head.

•

Q.   I have to pick a godmother for my daughter. Should I choose a good friend of limited financial means, or someone we're not very close to but who'll give my child expensive presents?

A.   Girls get two godmothers. Make sure she knows which one to impress.

•

Q.   Our next-door neighbor's children don't believe in Santa Claus and laugh every time our children bring him up. How can we make them stop?

A.   If your kids are that gullible, they deserve to be made fun of.

•

Q.   My friend's kid is a hopelessly spoiled only child. Would it be rude to tell the mother what I think?

A.   Poke a few pinholes in her diaphragm instead—the little brat could use some competition.

•

Q.   While I realize my daughter is exceptionally adorable, it annoys me when complete strangers come up and squeeze her cheeks or try to kiss her. Shouldn't they ask my permission before touching her?

A.   Paint a herpes sore on her mouth.

•

Q.   Parents tell me—often quite rudely—to mind my own business when I see a child being mistreated in public. But is it wrong to help prevent child abuse?

A.   Mind your own business.

•

Q. My mother-in-law keeps telling me how I should hold my baby daughter. How can I get her to lay off?

A. Hold the baby her way and pinch it till it screams.

•

Q. Is it necessary to send a baby present on receipt of a birth announcement?

A. No. Wait to see if the kid survives those first few months before you waste your money.

•

Q. Is there a polite way to inquire as to the gender of a new baby?

A. No.

•

Q. People frequently ask me whether my baby's going to be a boy or a girl, and act surprised that I haven't had any of those tests. Is this any of their business?

A. Obviously you look too old to be having a baby.

•

Q. Is it all right to bring a baby to a party?

A. Only if you cannot find a nice bottle of wine.

•

Q. My son served in Vietnam and brought a lovely wife home with him. Their three kids take after her, and when their dad is alone with them he's constantly encountering rude quips about their parentage. Is there a polite way to put an end to this?

A. If I were him, I'd be too embarrassed to take them out, unless it's to the lake for a good game of "Boat People."

•

Q. Piercing my little daughter's ears would be just too ethnic, but since she's still rather bald, people constantly mistake her for a boy. How can I politely correct them?

A. Tattoo a pink bow on her scalp.

•

Q. What's the best way to keep a yarmulke on a newborn who doesn't have much hair?

A. Staples.

•

Q. I have no problems about a mother breast-feeding in front of me, but I never know quite where to direct my gaze. Can you suggest a way I could feel more comfortable?

A. Put yourself at ease with small talk like, "Nice tits."

•

Q. Guests brought their six-month-old to a party without asking my permission, and the baby proceed to scream throughout the evening. How should I have reacted?

A. Fucking pissed off!

•

Q. Our child is clearly more advanced than our neighbors' of the same age. Must we pretend this is not the case?

A. Congratulate them on how much money they'll be saving on college tuition.

•

Q. Friends of ours are desperately trying to have kids, but the mother's just suffered her fifth miscarriage. I want to make sure my letter of condolence is in good taste. Do you have any pointers?

A. You should send a brief note saying, "You're getting pretty good at this," along with Billy Joel's "Only the Good Die Young," or Queen's "Another One Bites the Dust."

•

Q. When should a father stop undressing in front of his daughter?

A. When she starts giving him a hard-on, or insists on playing with his Cabbage Patch Snake.

•

Q. How soon after the baby's birth should announcements be sent out?

A. Anytime after you've counted the fingers and toes.

•

Q. I'm pregnant. My husband insists the baby assume his name and thinks I should too, but I don't agree. What can I say to get him off my back?

A. Tell him it's not his.

•

Q. The stream of visitors following our baby's birth really exhausted my wife and me, but we didn't know how to suggest that people cut their visits short. Any suggestions?

A. Serve formula.

•

Q. So many people seem to be having those tests run during pregnancy. Has this become a social necessity?

A. How else would they know to abort if it's a girl?

•

Q. My husband wants to videotape the birth of our child and show it to friends. Is this appropriate?

A. Yes, but a tape of you two screwing will be much more interesting—and could make you some mad money.

•

Q. I know this question doesn't belong in an etiquette book, but I'm so upset I have to ask. I just found out our pediatrician has AIDS—can my son catch it from him?

A. You bet. Of course, your son shouldn't be butt-fucking his doctor in the first place.

The Handicapped

Next time a handicapped person gets in your way, don't lose your temper. Remember, if it weren't for these folks, we'd never find parking places. Besides, you can afford to be polite to people in wheelchairs or on skateboards because they're so much shorter than you are. Just get those sticky questions out of the way early ("How'd you lose it?" "Can you still get it up?" "Does the twitching bother you?" "Does your dog really know what bathroom to take you to?"), and you'll be well on your way to having fun instead of just making fun.

Q. If they request help crossing the street, is it okay to ask blind people for money?

A. Yes, but wait until you're halfway across.

•

Q. Can paraplegics get it up? I have met a nice one through my church group and he has proposed, but I'd like to know just what I can expect out of it.

171

A.   I've *always* wondered the same thing. Please write back right after the honeymoon.

•

Q.   What kind of gift should I give my sightless brother for his graduation from Helen Keller College?

A.   A duck blind, a blind date, or how about a Venetian blind?

•

Q.   We live on the third floor of a four-floor walk-up and plan on having a dinner party. Unfortunately, one of the guests is confined to a wheelchair. Should we tell her about the stairs before she arrives?

A.   No. She may decline, and you'll miss watching her try to drag herself up the steps.

•

Q.   Who has the right-of-way, someone in a wheelchair or someone on crutches?

A.   Who cares?

•

Q.   My mother-in-law uses a walker to get around, but she's very careless and bangs into my furniture and all of our shins. Would it be rude to say something to her about her clumsiness?

A.   Yes. Wax the floors and put down little throw rugs instead.

•

Q. Our next-door neighbor's son is paralyzed from the neck down and his mother is constantly hinting to my kids about how lonely he is. I want to be kind, but what games could they possibly play with this boy?

A. Ringtoss. Prop up the kid's arms and legs. Award extra points for a head shot.

•

Q. I wanted to welcome the nice blind woman who just moved in next door, so I introduced myself and invited her over to "see my apartment sometime." Well, you can imagine how embarrassed I felt. Any suggestions for handling her actual visit more gracefully?

A. Just don't knock yourself out cleaning the place.

•

Q. A friend recently lost his right hand in an accident, and he's having some trouble adjusting to his metal prosthesis. For the time being, is it okay for him to extend his left hand during introductions?

A. Yes. By the way, how does he take a leak?

•

Q. My wife can't help falling to pieces when she goes to visit our mutilated son in the hospital. I know that situations like this require a supreme amount of tact. Should I say something?

A. No. Your son has to face the fact that he has become permanently repulsive to anyone but a plastic surgeon.

•

Q.   Should I feel guilty taking up a seat on the bus marked, "Reserved for the Handicapped"?

A.   No way. How are the cripples going to get on the bus in the first place?

•

Q.   I'm blind and prefer to get about by taxi, but others frequently beat me to them (I think). What can I do about this?

A.   Get a seeing-eye horse.

•

Q.   A friend of ours has a cleft palate and sprays us with spit whenever he talks. Should we say anything?

A.   No, but carry an umbrella whenever you're with him.

•

Q.   Why all the jokes about my growing bald spot? I don't point out to women that they're flat-chested or that they have thunder thighs.

A.   Why hold back?

•

Q.   I only have one arm and get embarrassed when invited out for dinner and something like steak is served. What should I do? Ask my hostess to cut it up for me? Say I'm a vegetarian? Try to cut the food with my good arm? Please help.

A.   Don't you have a claw or something?

•

Q.   Because of a back injury, I can't stand up straight or look people in the eyes when introducing myself. Many people find this behavior rude and think I'm doing it on purpose. How can I explain the problem?

A.   You can't. Find yourself an empty bell tower, or run for office—you'd make a perfect politician.

•

Q.   Should blind people wear their sunglasses inside?

A.   How're they going to know they're inside unless you tell them?

•

Q.   I'm paralyzed from the waist down. What should I do when a lady enters the room?

A.   Throw yourself on the floor.

•

Q.   I hired a handicapped man (he's paralyzed from the waist down) to head our personnel department, but he's just not working out. How do I let him go without his claiming discrimination?

A.   Tell him he's been chosen shortstop for the company softball team. Move his office to a higher floor so the elevator button is just out of reach. Keep an Out Of Order sign on the handicapped stall in the executive bathroom. Use your imagination.

•

Q.   Our handicapped office manager is leaving. Must we replace him with another disabled person?

A.   How about an Italian?

•

Q.   I'm under five feet tall and get quite claustrophobic when pushed to the back of a crowded elevator. What can I do to make people more considerate?

A.   Take the stairs, shortie.

Hospitals

If you think having a sick person at home is unpleasant, just visit someone in a hospital. The smell alone is enough to make you toss your cookies, even if you aren't the one queasy from chemotherapy. And all those tubes sticking out of orifices you haven't even tried *playing* with. Still, the fact that it's not you in traction or on kidney dialysis should help you cope. If the patient persists in describing his symptoms, aches, or incisions, remind him he's behaving in very poor taste. And leave. After all, etiquette in the hospital is more for your benefit than for the patient, because it allows you to make your visit as brief as possible.

━━━━━━━━━━

Q.   My friend is terminally ill in the hospital and refuses to see me. What should I do?

A.   Get-well cards are always in good taste. Make it cheerful and fun with bunnies and ducks.

•

Q.   My husband's a doctor, and patients are forever calling up in the middle of the night with the most minor complaints. Is there any way to put an end to this thoughtless behavior?

A.   Get an answering machine that says, "Take two aspirin and call me in the morning" or "Give billing address before stating your complaint."

•

Q.   I can never tell who's in charge on the hospital floor where my husband is recuperating without looking like a fool. How can I find out?

A.   You can always tell the head nurse by the dirt on her knees.

•

Q.   I do volunteer work at the local hospital and would like to cheer up some terminally ill gay patients with a small party. What should I serve?

A.   Kool-AIDS.

•

Q.   My lover has AIDS and is confined to the hospital. What kind of present could I bring to cheer him up?

A.   Something perishable, like a fruit salad.

•

Q.   A friend of ours, a former champion equestrian, is now in the hospital with lung cancer. What can I bring to brighten his day—he led such an active life?

A.   A saddle for his iron lung.

•

Q.   What should I do if a friend I'm visiting in the hospital starts to smoke?

A.   Throw water on her or smother her in a blanket.

•

Q.   When is euthanasia socially acceptable?

A.   When the hospital costs outweigh the pleasure of the patient's company.

•

Q.   Why is it so damn hard to get a doctor to give you the facts? During a recent hospital stay, it was like pulling teeth to get the slightest bit of information about my prognosis from any of the staff. Is it proper to confront someone on the medical staff?

A.   Have you made out your will?

•

Q.   My roommate sustained a terrible concussion and may have brain damage. What kind of gift would make his hospital stay more comfortable?

A.   Mr. Potato Head.

•

Q.   My cousin is understandably depressed after undergoing a colostomy, since her intestines are now hitched up to this yucky little sack. What can I get her that would cheer her up?

A.   How about shoes to match the bag?

•

Q.   I'm sharing a semiprivate room with an elderly man who describes his barium enema in detail to each of his many visitors. May I tell him to shut up already?

A.   Sure. Just don't tell him he's full of shit.

•

Q.   I'm known as a bit of a klutz, but isn't my sick friend taking it too far? He says he's afraid to ask me to visit him in the hospital because I might trip over the cords of his life-support system.

A.   Can you blame him?

•

Q.   A good friend is dying of cancer but I can't force myself to go visit her in the hospital. The entire scene freaks me out.

A.   Same here.

•

Q.   Is it impolite to inquire as to the nature of someone's illness or operation?

A.   No. Come right out and ask, "So, does Jim have cancer?" or "Was that a hysterectomy Naomi went in for?" Think of the nasty and inaccurate gossip you're sparing the family.

•

Q.   Why must people be so rude about my husband's upcoming hemorrhoids operation? They wouldn't think it was so funny if he were having open-heart surgery.

A.   True, but he's not. There's a big difference between an affair of the heart and a pain in the ass.

•

Q.   Is there any way to deal with people overstaying their welcome during a hospital visit?

A.   Call the nurse and tell her the enema is about to kick in.

Old Age

Nervous about dumping on the elderly when you might be one too someday, shuffling feebly to the bank to cash your Social Security check? Lighten up —today's old fogies won't be around to remember how you treated them, or they'll be too senile to know what number to call for help. Your parents dumped on you, right?

The key thing is to keep any old folks from moving in—it's so much easier to be halfway decent to someone you don't live with. If it's unavoidable, keep the phone out of reach and limit mobility with stairs or slippery little rugs. Remind them frequently that if it weren't for you, they'd be sitting in dirty diapers at the state home. They'll behave, or else . . .

———

Q. My grandfather has lost control of his bodily functions and frequently soils himself. What should we do?

A. Stand back.

•

Q. Is it proper to place my false teeth next to the bed at night?

A. Yes, if you're about to give a gum job.

•

Q. After dinner, my great-aunt always takes out her teeth and puts them on her plate while she sips her tea. Is this permitted at the table?

A. Only if you consider picking your nose with a fork proper table manners.

•

Q. My grandfather is hard of hearing and assumes everyone else is, too. He's always shouting, even when you're sitting right next to him. Should I say something to him?

A. No, you should shout something to him.

•

Q. I've had it. Yesterday I tried to help a little old lady across the street and she told me to fuck off! Well, never again. I'm so angry I feel like punching the next old lady I see right in the face. So what do you think of that?

A. Go for it! Behavior like that pisses me off, too.

•

Q. Father is in a local nursing home. Four of his five children live nearby, but I seem to be the only one who manages a visit more than once a month. How can I let them know how rude their behavior is?

A. Unless you're in line for a substantial inheritance, why knock yourself out?

•

Q. Our mother has been diagnosed as having Alzheimer's disease and is increasingly confused and unable to care for herself. Whose responsibility is it to find a nursing home for her?

A. Why do you care? She's not going to remember who put her there.

•

Q. My grandmother still has all her marbles, but is increasingly incontinent. This is embarrassing to all concerned, not to mention hard on the rugs. What can be done?

A. Train Granny to stay on the linoleum.

•

Q. I commute to work by subway, and almost every morning some gray-haired old lady shoves her way through the car, stepping on my toes and kicking me in the shins. (It's worse when they're wielding umbrellas or canes.) I'm fed up but don't know what to do.

A. Try tripping them up near the edge of the platform just as the train comes in.

•

Q. Our mother will be eighty years old next week and is healthy except for a weak heart. Can you suggest a quiet yet fun event to celebrate the occasion?

A. If she's well off, throw a surprise party.

•

Q. Should I say anything to my grandfather when he accidentally wets himself? He's very old.

A. Pamper® him instead.

•

Q. Once a week I drive these two ancient sisters around town to do their errands. I swear one of them's got the hots for me—she's always winking or eyeing my crotch. What's a polite way to deal with the problem?

A. Don't knock a gum job till you've tried it.

•

Q. I dread each morning because I'm afraid my great-grandfather, who is terribly frail, hasn't survived the night. Is there some way to check on his health without worrying him?

A. Try throwing cold water on him and seeing if he reacts.

•

Q. My mother is worth a bundle and doesn't believe in wills. She also suffers from Alzheimer's disease. How can I get what's rightfully mine without appearing too crass?

A. Write up a will in her name and tell her she must have forgotten about it. If she gives you any shit, threaten to commit her.

•

Q. My grandfather and I have opposing political views. If I disagree with one of his absurd statements, can I tell him what I think, or should I keep my opinions to myself?

A.   Unless you owe him money or hope to borrow some, get it off your chest.

•

Q.   We are planning a seventieth birthday party for my dad, who has emphysema. At his age, is it still proper to have candles on the cake?

A.   Sure. Go for the joke kind that relight themselves, and see how long it takes till he passes out.

•

Q.   My in-laws both have hearing problems, so our long-distance conversations become hopelessly garbled and frustrating for everyone. But I feel terrible if I don't keep in touch. What's the polite thing to do?

A.   Leave well enough alone.

•

Q.   I find those old bag ladies a terrible eyesore and am particularly disturbed when they panhandle. What can I do to discourage them from bothering me?

A.   Try a can of gasoline and a Bic lighter.

Nasty Habits

There is no such thing as a bad habit. The problem arises when people let habits bother them. We'd be much better off if we picked our noses with pride, farted with elan, and burped with aplomb.

And why all this noise about smoking? Are you going to stop screwing because you might catch AIDS or herpes? Of course not. Those anti-smokers, especially the born-again variety, are the ones who need lessons in etiquette. How dare they tell me I can't smoke in a restaurant or on a plane? Hell, a good cigar is better than a mediocre blow job. So fuck all of you and give me a light.

Q. What can I do to prevent myself from perspiring? I'm mortified at the thought of turning off Mr. Right.

A. Don't move. Stand perfectly still.

•

Q.   I know I shouldn't pick my nose, but how else can I clean it?

A.   Hire someone.

•

Q.   What should one do with a tissue once it has been used?

A.   Throw it out, jerk.

•

Q.   I know that if I have to burp, I should cover my mouth with my hand, but what should I do if I have to fart?

A.   Cover your ass with your fist.

•

Q.   I've found myself in an embarrassing situation a number of times. I'm with a girl I really want to impress, but I have to pass gas. What can I do if this problem crops up again?

A.   Implode.

•

Q.   If someone in a group cuts a really smelly fart, should I say something?

A.   Absolutely not. Haven't you heard the old adage, "He who dealt it, smelled it"?

•

Q. Is it bad manners to clip your nails in public?

A. No. But it's easier to pick your nose.

•

Q. What should I do if my crotch starts to itch in a public place?

A. Scratch it, silly. Then scratch mine.

•

Q. My mother always told us not to comb our hair in the kitchen. Is this really a breach of etiquette?

A. Only if your hair's a different color from the main dish.

•

Q. Where is the best place to pick dirt and grime from between one's toes without causing any public offense?

A. Cleveland.

•

Q. My wife has the disgusting habit of picking her nose and eating what she finds. Of course she isn't so gross as to excavate in public, but she thinks it's okay to do it at home. How can I dissuade her from this nauseating activity?

A. Don't knock it until you've tried it.

•

Q. When is spitting permissible?

A. When words aren't enough.

•

Q. I hate sanctimonious nonsmokers who have just kicked the habit. Is there a polite way to tell them to buzz off and leave us smokers in peace?

A. "Mind your own fucking business!" usually works for me.

•

Q. My father and I both smoke, but since he's just been diagnosed as having lung cancer, should I refrain from smoking in his presence?

A. You don't have cancer yet—why should you suffer?

•

Q. My friends laugh at me because, although I don't smoke, I carry a lighter in case I meet a lady who needs a light. What's wrong with this?

A. Do you carry tampons too?

•

Q. Is it impolite to eavesdrop?

A. Only if you're caught.

•

Q. I love dunking doughnuts or cookies in my coffee. Is this socially acceptable behavior?

A. Yes. Myself, I enjoy dunking small kittens in the bathtub.

•

Q.   A friend of ours loves to use big words—he thinks it makes him seem smarter or something. We're getting really sick of this habit and want to do something. How would Blanche handle it?

A.   Defenestrate him.

•

Q.   Is it socially acceptable to say "Bless you" to a stranger?

A.   Yes, if you're Jesus Christ.

•

Q.   I find the blaring of those huge portable radios very annoying, especially when it's that "rap" music. Shouldn't the offenders (usually a pack of black kids) be prohibited from playing them in public places?

A.   Absolutely. *You* tell them.

•

Q.   My fiancé has terrible body odor. Should I tell him to use a more powerful deodorant or what?

A.   He sounds Italian. Tell him to change his underwear more than once a week.

•

Q.   My husband loves to pass gas and isn't the least bit embarrassed. Is this proper social behavior?

A.   Don't be so uptight. A highly audible fart can turn a boring, stuffy affair into a laff riot.

Introductions

How many times have you been placed in the awkward situation of not knowing the name or position of the person you're talking to? You pretend to recall, but it's hopeless. You break into a cold sweat, lose track of the conversation, begin to tremble. Why? Because you've been brought up to consider your lapse of memory as rude and thoughtless.

What a waste of energy. Think about it: if they remember you and you can't recall ever meeting them, obviously you're the person with the power. Flaunt it. Say, "I'm sorry, but you're too insignificant for me to recall your name." Remember, a good defense is an offense.

Q. Yesterday I was introduced to a double amputee (the arms), and was perfectly mortified when I instinctively went to shake hands. Is there a proper way to handle such an introduction?

A. Yes. Pat his or her right stump gently, repress that shudder of revulsion, and say, "Pleased to meet you."

•

Q.   What's the correct response when people come up and greet you like long-lost relatives and you don't have the faintest idea who they are?

A.   "Who the fuck are *you* and what do you want?"

•

Q.   What is the correct way to address a Cardinal of the Roman Catholic Church?

A.   "Here, birdy, birdy, birdy."

•

Q.   When telephoning a new acquaintance, should I say, "Hello, Mrs. Smith, this is Mary," or "Hi, June, this is Mary"?

A.   It doesn't matter, unless the person is named neither Mrs. Smith nor June and as long as your name is Mary.

•

Q.   My husband and I have been invited to a diplomatic reception in honor of the ruler of Namibia. How should we address him when introduced?

A.   "Yo, King."

•

Q.   Do I really have to stand up when little old ladies come into the room?

A.   No.

•

Q. I'm having a black-tie dinner party for some very influential Washington types. A couple of the guests are black multimillionaire diplomats. How should I address them—Mr.——? Sir——? Your Excellency?

A. Try "Tycoon."

•

Q. I've been given a letter of introduction to an important diplomat, but unfortunately the author of the letter died before I had time to use it. What should I do?

A. Add a P.S. requesting that the reader supply you with an audience, room and board, spending money, etc.

•

Q. My name is Alicia, but people are always calling me Alice. How can I correct them without embarrassing them?

A. That's what you get for having a fancy-schmancy name like Alicia. Change it to Alice.

•

Q. I can't remember names for the life of me. I've tried every kind of mnemonic device, but I still go blank when the moment of truth arrives and I end up embarrassing myself. What should I do so people don't think me rude?

A. Blame it on Alzheimer's.

•

Q. I have a problem. At many of the parties I attend, the people wear name tags to facilitate introductions. I see nothing wrong with this except for the placement of the tags. I get so embarrassed when I try to meet a young woman and I must stare at her bosom in order to read her name. What can be done?

A.   You call that a problem?

•

Q.   When is it appropriate to kiss a woman on the lips on the first meeting?

A.   After sex, unless she just went down on you.

•

Q.   Is it appropriate to introduce people by just their first names?

A.   Why—are two names too much for you?

•

Q.   A friend and I are co-hosting a party and are afraid people won't mingle. Should we have them wear name tags?

A.   Only nerds wear name tags.

•

Q.   At an informal party in our house, may I rely on the guests to introduce themselves?

A.   Yes, but you'll have more fun if you invite people you know.

•

Q.   At what age should you start addressing a woman as
"Mrs." instead of "Miss"?

A.   When she starts looking too old to bag a husband.

•

Q.   I was very embarrassed when I met my gynecologist
at a party and he didn't recognize me. What should I have
done?

A.   Spread 'em.

Social Correspondence

Wasting your time on a stupid note that's just going to get lost in the mail? Why do you think the phone was invented? You don't even have to know how to spell anymore, as long as you can dial.

If you insist on putting it on paper, don't be intimidated by some ridiculous Frog expression like R.S.V.P. Show up with a bunch of friends, and fuck the hostess if she can't take a joke. As for thank-you notes, I don't know what all the fuss is about. If you like the present, say thank you; if not, don't bother.

———

Q. Should a ransom note be typed or handwritten? Please reply promptly. Or else.

A. Neither. A note composed of words and letters pieced together from various newspapers and magazines will make for more festive reading and a much better souvenir of the occasion.

•

Q. Are there any do's and don'ts to keep in mind when composing a ransom note?

A. DO: Make your demands specific.
Cut out words from magazines with easy-to-read type.
Use paste instead of Scotch tape.
Check your grammar.

DON'T: Sign your real name. (A simple "A Friend" will do.)

•

Q. Is it correct to write a thank-you note to the accounting department when I receive my paycheck?

A. Yes, if you have absolutely nothing better to do.

•

Q. Do I send a thank-you note to a woman after sleeping with her? It was a one-night stand.

A. Only if she swallowed.

•

Q. Is one obliged to send a thank-you note after spending a weekend with the in-laws?

A. No, unless you actually want to be asked back.

•

Q. How soon after receipt of a gift must a thank-you note be sent?

A. After it's been opened and before it's returned.

•

Q.   How do you thank someone who's presented you with a gift of truly astounding generosity?

A.   Say, "Okay, what do I have to do for it?"

•

Q.   I have a large family. Is it impolite to send Xerox copies of my letters to several people?

A.   Address and sign each individually. If the Xerox is good enough, they may never find out.

•

Q.   I have just taken on a pen pal who is a prison inmate, and I'm not sure how to address him. "Dear Jim" seems a bit familiar, but "Dear Inmate #38914429" seems rather formal. What would be correct?

A.   Try "Dear 3891."

•

Q.   When declining an invitation, must I give the reason why?

A.   No, but if pushed, make it clear you got a better offer.

•

Q.   Although I wasn't invited to a friend's last party, I feel that inviting her to mine would avoid any social unease later on. Don't you agree?

A.   What are you, a masochist?

•

Q.   I accepted an invitation before realizing that the party coincided with the last episode of *Dallas*. I haven't missed a show yet. What can I do?

A.   Spring for a VCR, cheapskate.

•

Q.   Can I read a postcard addressed to somebody else?

A.   I give up, can you?

•

Q.   What's the correct format for a suicide note?

A.   Write the date and time on the upper right-hand corner (this will assist the coroner). Address it "To whom it may concern."
     A brief sentence covering each point below should suffice:

        (1) why you're upset;
        (2) who's to blame;
        (3) and whether you're leaving anything behind.

Write your full name at the bottom of the note to assist in identification. Salutations are not necessary; neither is postage, nor return address.

Miscellaneous Queries

Okay, so maybe without Blanche's help you could've figured out which fork to use or what to wear to the funeral. But what about those annoying bits of protocol that slip between the cracks: how to register at a sleazy motel, prevent people with weird hairdos from sitting in front of you at the movies, and keep your neighbors guessing about your sex life. Read on and you'll never get caught with your pants down. Or if you do, at least you'll know how to enjoy it.

Q. I'm sick to death of rich bitches who sashay into the store and treat us salesgirls like dirt. Shouldn't they show some manners too?

A. Why waste them on anyone making minimum wage?

•

Q. It seems that whenever I'm really in need of a salesman, he disappears or becomes deaf. Should this be brought to the attention of the store manager, or should I just wait patiently?

201

A.   Take advantage of the excellent shoplifting oppor-
tunities.

•

Q.   What is the proper way to answer a phone?

A.   Remove the handset from the cradle.

•

Q.   As I don't want to be rude, I have a difficult time
getting rid of sales representatives over the telephone. Do
you have any suggestions?

A.   Hand the receiver to a small child.

•

Q.   Is it polite to ask who's calling when the phone rings
at home?

A.   Only if you're deeply in debt or sell drugs for a living.

•

Q.   Most of my friends have answering machines, but
many delight in recording obnoxiously long messages.
What appropriate message would you suggest?

A.   "What do you want?" BEEP.

•

Q.   If a friend is late in paying back a loan, is there a
polite way to remind him of his debt?

A.   If you're Italian, break his legs. If you're Jewish,
charge interest. If you're Polish, forget whom you lent it
to. And if you're a WASP, please don't bring it up again.

•

Q. I'm an interior decorator, and it irritates me every time people assume I'm gay. Shouldn't they mind their own damn business?

A. My, my, aren't we testy.

•

Q. I can't stand it when people are inconsiderate enough to talk during a movie. What's the best way of getting them to shut up?

A. Why do you think Milk Duds were invented?

•

Q. What's a polite way of discouraging people who've already seen the movie from telling you what's going to happen onscreen just before it does?

A. "Will you please shut the fuck up." (Unfortunately, Milk Duds are not effective at close range.)

•

Q. During intermission at the movies, is it okay for the man to leave the woman alone?

A. Yes. If she's exceedingly ugly, he can leave while the lights are still out.

•

Q. Isn't it awfully rude to talk in the movies?

A. Not if you've seen it before.

•

Q. When should I say, "Excuse me," and when should I say, "Pardon me"?

A. Use "Pardon me" when addressing a governor, and "Excuse me" to everyone else. Check with Miss Manners.

•

Q. I hate being stopped on the street by people wanting to know the time, or how to get to such-and-such an address. How can I tell them to leave me alone?

A. I'm busy. Ask Amy Vanderbilt.

•

Q. What's the difference between a "vase" and a "vahz"?

A. About fifty bucks.

•

Q. Is it appropriate to applaud after watching three or four people fuck each other on stage at those live sex shows?

A. Yes. I refer to it as giving them the clap, and do recommend it after an exceptional performance.

•

Q. Sexist and ethnic jokes truly offend me. What should I say to people who find it amusing to tell these kinds of jokes in my presence?

A. You're asking the wrong person, but thanks for buying the book, sucker.

What do you call a series of books that will have you groaning with laughter?

Blanche Knott's **Truly Tasteless Jokes**

Over 3 million copies of Truly Tasteless Jokes in print!

TRULY TASTELESS JOKES IV
_____ 90365-0 $2.95 U.S.   _____ 90366-9 $3.50 Can.

TRULY TASTELESS JOKES V
_____ 90371-5 $2.95 U.S.   _____ 90372-3 $3.50 Can.

TRULY TASTELESS JOKES VI
_____ 90361-8 $2.95 U.S.   _____ 90373-1 $3.75 Can.

THE TRULY TASTELESS JOKE-A-DATE BOOK 1987
Spiral bound for easy access to a laugh a day!
_____ 90485-1 $3.95 U.S.   _____ 90523-8 $4.95 Can.

BLANCHE KNOTT'S BOOK OF TRULY TASTELESS ETIQUETTE
Bad taste for *all* occasions!
_____ 90590-4 $3.50 U.S.   _____ 90591-2 $4.50 Can.

ST. MARTIN'S PRESS—MAIL SALES
175 Fifth Avenue, New York, NY 10010

Please send me the book(s) I have checked above. I am enclosing a check or money order (not cash) for $_____ plus 75¢ per order to cover postage and handling (New York residents add applicable sales tax).

Name _____

Address_____

City _____ State_____ Zip Code_____
Allow at least 4 to 6 weeks for delivery